# The Last One Standing

'I rode out beneath the soft moonlight, with a single intent, to kill a man.'

In the Territories one man is more evil and terrible than all others. From murdering Chinese immigrant workers on the Transcontinental Railroad to slaughtering anyone who dares beat him at cards, Moose Schmidt kills and maims for no other reason than to enjoy the surge of control and power it gives him.

Callum Johnson's father was killed by Moose Schmidt when Callum was a young boy. Now it is payback time. Teaming up with his father's old Cherokee scout and a beautiful Chinese girl, Callum ventures deep into Moose Schmidt's territory seeking justice and revenge.

But Moose Schmidt has eyes and ears across the land. He knows Callum is coming and he is ready and waiting. And determined to have fun killing the young man.

Armed with just a six gun and the lessons his father taught him, can Callum and his companions succeed where even the greatest bounty hunters have failed?

# The Last One Standing

Derek Rutherford

A Black Horse Western

ROBERT HALE

© Derek Rutherford 2019
First published in Great Britain 2019


ISBN 978-0-7198-3017-4


The Crowood Press
The Stable Block
Crowood Lane
Ramsbury
Marlborough
Wiltshire SN8 2HR

www.bhwesterns.com

Robert Hale is an imprint
of The Crowood Press


The right of Derek Rutherford to be identified as
author of this work has been asserted by him
in accordance with the Copyright, Designs and
Patents Act 1988

Typeset by
Derek Doyle & Associates, Shaw Heath
Printed and bound in Great Britain by
4Bind Ltd, Stevenage, SG1 2XT

**1**

**Indian Territory 1875**

My father was Samuel Johnson. He was a big and fearless man, and for many years he brought outlaws back from the Indian Territory and handed them over to the authorities, usually to hang. Unless he brought them back already dead, which happened occasionally. Sam Johnson liked to fight, he liked to drink, and he loved women. He had reputations for all three vices. But he also had a weakness for believing that there was good in all people – even wanted men – and that's what got him killed.

Sam was on the trail of a fellow by the name of Moose Schmidt. There was, reputedly, nothing good about Moose at all. He was a known killer. A cruel man who liked to inflict pain simply to enjoy the surge of power it gave him. Several authorities had warrants out for Moose, but my father wasn't working for any of them. A Chinese woman who had come to New York from England and had travelled as far west as Natchez had employed my father to bring her Moose Schmidt.

Back then I didn't know what the Chinese lady wanted with Schmidt. I only knew that my father took me all the way to Natchez with him, and in the stifling heat we drank iced tea, watched painted riverboats, and met the Chinese woman, who was the most exotic person I had ever seen.

Ten days later, after a long ride home from Natchez, my father spent a cordial evening with my mother and I at home in St Mary's Gap. They were in love, and yet often couldn't stand the sight of each other. Leastways, my mother couldn't stand the sight of Sam Johnson. I don't think he ever had that trouble with her. He always had an eye for a pretty woman and my mother was as pretty as they come. Trouble was she could see all those other pretty women in his eyes and no matter how much she loved him, she hated him too.

In the morning he lit out for Fort Smith and it was the last time we saw him alive.

Those days my father travelled with a Cherokee scout by the name of One Leg Hawk. One Leg was in a bad way when he told me the story of how Moose Schmidt had killed my father. One Leg was in that hinterland where, for a couple of days and nights, life and death tried to outbid each other for his soul.

'Schmidt asked to see his boy,' One Leg told me,

his voice barely more than a whisper. 'Or at least one of his boys. They say he had many scattered around.'

We were in the Agent's office in Green Springs on the eastern edge of the territories. It wasn't but a day's ride from there to St Mary's Gap and two men had arrived the previous afternoon to pass on the news about my father. I'd left my mother crying and cursing in equal measure and I rode back with the messengers, driving our flatbed on which to bring my father's body home. By the time I'd got to the Agent's office, which was a white brick building as nice on the outside as anything in St Mary's, the doctor had already dug a bullet from the side of One Leg's chest and another from his shoulder. He was bandaged up and he was lying on blankets close to the kitchen stove despite it being summer. He was shivering and he was sweating and he stank of the whiskey they'd poured on him and into him while the doc operated.

'Schmidt said he knew it would be the last time,' One Leg said to me, grimacing as a spasm of pain ripped through him. 'But the least your father could do was to grant him that much. "Just let me give him one last handshake",' Schmidt said.

' "How old is this boy of yours?" your father asked.

'Schmidt said, "He's five years old".'

'Your father said, "Then you should give him a

hug, not a handshake." '

The way One Leg told it, Schmidt's boy was a breed who was living with his mother, a Choctaw, not more than a half day's ride from where my father had captured Schmidt. Schmidt was tied up and he had a resigned look on his face. One Leg estimated Schmidt was in his forties by then. 'It looked like all the fight had gone out of him,' One Leg said. 'Too many years running.'

So my father had taken a diversion to allow a defeated man one last hug with his boy.

'*He* knew,' One Leg said. 'And I knew. And of course your father knew, that you couldn't hug someone if your own hands were tied up. So that moment was coming when we were going to have to untie Schmidt.'

It happened in a dirt clearing next to a wooden hut where the Choctaw woman and Schmidt's boy lived. Out front a pot was suspended over a fire, bubbling and smelling pretty good for Choctaw food, One Leg said. Three dogs lay in the shade. When the men rode up the dogs started whimpering. As Schmidt climbed down from his horse the dogs slunk away around the back of the hut.

It was around midday, maybe an hour past, and the air was hot and still. The dust from the horses hung in the air and dried the men's throats and there were lizards basking on a pile of rocks that the Choctaw woman had cleared to make a small vegetable patch.

She stood in the doorway of the hut, no expression on her face, no smile, not even any acknowledgement. 'If she did anything,' One Leg said, 'it was just to nod slightly as if she had been expecting this moment for a very long time.'

Then she turned and said something into the hut and a moment later Schmidt's boy appeared by the side of her legs. He was dressed in western clothes – a loose-fitting shirt and blue pants, and he was wearing tan moccasins. His hair was jet black and his eyes were as hard as his mother's.

Schmidt crouched down to the boy's level and held out his hands – still tied – in front of him. He smiled and called to his son. But before the boy moved Schmidt turned, rising up to his full height again, and he held his tied wrists towards my father.

'Two minutes,' Schmidt said.

My father untied the knots and then he took a step backwards, easing his gun from his holster. One Leg, up there on his horse, already had his rifle lowered and was pointing it at Schmidt's belly. Schmidt's own Navy Colt was back on my father's horse, buried deep in a bag.

'Thank you,' Schmidt said. He smiled and he turned back to his son, crouching down again, holding his arms wide open now.

The boy ran into Schmidt's arms, smiling. Even his mother smiled then.

'They must have tucked the gun into the back of the boy's pants,' One Leg said. 'Schmidt hugged his son, and in the same movement he stood up, holding the boy like a shield so neither your father nor I dared shoot, and there was a gun in his hand and he didn't even blink. That gun blazed, once, twice, three times.'

All three bullets hit my father. One in the throat, one in the heart, and one in the eye. Any one of those bullets would have killed him.

One Leg couldn't shoot back because of the boy. But the fact that Schmidt had been so determined to kill my father that he'd done it three times gave One Leg the split second he needed to turn, to crouch, to spur his horse. To run.

But Schmidt was quick and two of his bullets still ploughed into One Leg and those bullets almost knocked the scout from his horse. Somehow One Leg held on. The last bullet from Schmidt's gun left a hole in One Leg's hat and a crease along his hairline but it didn't even draw blood.

'By the time a couple of marshals made it back there Schmidt and the Choctaw and the boy were gone,' One Leg said. 'They'd taken your father's horse, too. But he was still lying there in the dust and the dogs were beside him, looking at your father's body and wondering, I guess, if it was safe to eat him.'

That's how my father got killed.

I was fourteen.

**2**

The way it was out there in the Territory, if you kept your ear to the ground you could pretty much follow a man around. I don't mean track him, the way a good scout like One Leg Hawk would track him; I mean hear stories about him, and follow him through those stories.

Moose Schmidt killed a man in Gentry when I was fifteen. It was over a game of cards, supposedly. The story was that Moose called the man out for cheating, but the fellow – and all the other players – were adamant that he hadn't been. Nevertheless, Moose was so mad that the fellow said, 'OK, you say I'm cheating, I say I'm not. You take your money back, despite the fact I won it fair and square, and I'm gone. Nothing I hate more than a sore loser.' But Moose wasn't interested in the money. He was in the mood for killing someone and he followed the fellow out onto the street and called him a cheat and a thief and he insulted the fellow's mother and eventually the man had no choice but to draw, and that was when Moose shot him dead.

When I was sixteen Moose hanged two fellows he insisted had been trying to steal his horse when he was camping in the wilds north of Broken Arrow. The story was Moose actually forced one of the men to hang the other in exchange for allowing the first man to go free. After the fellow had hanged his partner, Moose, of course, reneged on the deal. Later the same year he shot dead a man he said had been getting ready to rape an Indian squaw. I was seventeen when I heard a story from a little further north about how Moose cut off a man's thumbs when the man refused a gunfight. Moose said the fellow had stolen money from him. There was no one to deny it, or at least, there was no one prepared to stand up and deny it. They said Moose gave the fellow chance to apologize for the stealing between cutting each thumb off. One story said there were three hours between the two thumbs.

It seemed to me, from the stories that I heard, that it wasn't just the killing and maiming with Moose, but it was the manner of the acts. It was as if he enjoyed them so much he wanted to make the moments last.

When I was almost eighteen, there came word about how Moose Schmidt had shot dead a very exotic and beautiful Chinese lady. He shot her in the back, they said. And he did so because he was scared.

I followed Moose through these stories, and many other tales too, because one day I was determined to set out to kill Moose Schmidt.

My mother ran a small boarding house in St Mary's Gap. St Mary's was getting to be like a proper town. A whole row of brick buildings had been raised, entrepreneurs were setting up all sorts of shops and concerns, there was even a small theatre being constructed. Business at the boarding house was generally brisk. A lot of men figured that a pretty woman on her own might be in need of a good man. They were wrong, and most of them weren't good men, anyway. Not that they were bad. Not bad like Moose Schmidt. But they didn't always have a whole lot going for them. They came and they stayed for a while and if they didn't find a way of making a go of things in St Mary's then on they drifted. If they did find a way of making regular money, then they usually also found a permanent place in which to live. I helped out keeping the place fixed up. I also worked with horses down at the livery and I learned to break them, too, over at Crawford's ranch. I used to light out for days and nights at a time, hunting. I shot rabbits and deer and coyote and once a wolf, all with a Springfield musket that my pa had given me. He told me it had belonged to a Confederate soldier. I bought myself an Army Colt, too, and I practised the hell out of that thing.

13

I recall my father showing me how I could make paper cartridges. Until that lesson it had been a laborious process loading that gun. First of all you had to make sure the chamber was clean, then pour in just the right amount of gunpowder. Luckily the powder flask that came with the gun always dispensed a perfect measure. After that came the wadding which one would compress down tight against the powder using the ramrod lever below the gun barrel. Then came the ball itself, which was also rammed into place. Do all of that five times, then for each of those loaded chambers place a percussion cap on the nipple at the back of the cylinder and you were good to go.

Sam Johnson taught me early – probably before I even had my own gun – that you always left one chamber empty, and that was the chamber you rested the hammer on when you were riding, or walking, or just going about your daily business.

I think I asked, the way a young boy would, what happened if you were up against six men? If you'd only loaded five chambers then how were you going to kill the sixth man?

My father didn't mention the obvious flaws in my question – how likely was it that you were ever going to be up against six men? And if you were, was another bullet really going to make a difference? He did show me how to fan the hammer on that gun, though. Just in case, he said, I was ever up against five men. But he also explained the benefit of the empty chamber.

'Your horse lands heavily and the shock goes all the way through you, doesn't it?' he said to me. 'Well your gun feels it too, and if the hammer is resting on a loaded chamber that shock can be enough to discharge that bullet. You could shoot your horse accidentally. You could shoot yourself accidentally. Just because your horse landed heavily.'

It was another day that he showed me the paper cartridges. I recall him sitting at the kitchen table first demonstrating how to clean the gun. Ma was in the background sort of glaring at him, but also smiling because the moment, in its own way, was nice. And pretty rare, too.

After we'd got done on the cleaning, my father showed me how to roll and load a paper cartridge. He said back in the war the soldiers were given prepacked boxes of such cartridges, and when I got rich I could buy those myself. But in the meantime knowing how to roll them would save me time. And it certainly did. Once I got the hang of it I would take a tin of those handmade cartridges up in the woods and practise fan-shooting that pistol like Samuel Johnson had showed me. Over and over.

Years later, when I had just turned eighteen, my ma – having watched my endless gun work – said, 'When you find him, you kill him straight away. You don't talk and you don't ask questions, and you don't get to wondering on anything. You just shoot him like he did your father. Then you come home.'

I almost said that I didn't know what she was talking about, but the look in her eyes told me she knew more about me than I knew about myself.

'He's way up north, at the moment,' I said. It didn't mean I wasn't ready to go. It was just my way of saying, 'Thanks, Ma.'

I figured the time was only weeks away. I was a pretty good shot now, and I was as quick on the draw as anyone I'd seen. But before I could set off another Chinese lady came into my life.

# 3

I was in the King's Arms drinking whiskey and water at the long bar when Lin Wu Jia walked in and stood next to me. I glanced across without really focusing and saw a dusty cowboy, a brown hat pulled low, a red neckerchief, and a mustard-coloured coat that was white in patches with salt and dust. The coat was unbuttoned and revealed a navy pin-striped vest and blue work trousers. I returned to my whiskey but the quick glance at the cowboy had left a residual image in my mind. The cowboy had dark and beautiful almond-shaped eyes, red lips and smooth perfect skin.

I looked into the mirror at the back of the bar.

The mirror was cracked and the silver was coming off in places. There was a shelf running the length of it on which bottles and glasses and clay mugs blocked the reflection.

But I could see the cowboy was looking at me.

I turned and now I saw that the cowboy was a girl,

an Eastern girl no less. Eastern as in Chinese, although I didn't know such specifics until a minute or so later. Even with the hat and scarf covering some of her face, I could see that she was beautiful.

She smiled and said, 'You're Callum Johnson.'

*She knew me.*

Jimmy Stephens was at the far end of the bar talking to Lazy Lowe Holland and Two-Bit Tony who made their living bringing in goods from Chicago. They weren't particular; you wanted guns, beans, whiskey, wheels, ribbons, glass, soap, *anything*, they'd source and ship it. Rumour had it that old Avery Latcham had them bring in a young wife for him. I'm not sure how true that was, but Avery did have a pretty wife these days and I don't believe she could speak more than ten words of English, so how he won her over, if indeed Lazy and Two-Bit hadn't been involved, I had no idea. Jimmy Stephens owned the Kings Head. He was from England and did his best to make the bar as much like an old English inn as he could. That was probably what he was talking about now, discussing with Lazy and Two-Bit on whether or not they could find some more items to add to the brass hunting horns and cane fishing rods he had hanging on the wall.

Jimmy Stephens looked up, saw the cowboy – the cow*girl*, but I don't think he'd cottoned on to that yet – and started coming towards us.

'Who are you?' I asked her, still reeling from her knowing my name.

'I'm Lin Wu Jia.' As she said her name she bowed very slightly, just a dip of the head.

Jimmy Stephens was half way along the bar now. A fellow by the name of Dovetail Dave who managed a small carpentry business held out his glass and Jimmy paused to refill it.

'How do you know me?'

'You met my mother once.' Her English was very good, although mother did sound a little like *mudder*. She had an accent, but it was subtle, as if she'd worked hard to lose it.

I'd only ever met one Chinese lady before, so I knew who her mother was, and now a hundred questions filled my head. How had she found me? *Why* had she found me? Was this to do with my father? Her mother?

But Jimmy was heading our way again.

'I'm not sure you should be in here,' I said.

'Why? They don't allow women?'

I paused and she saw in my eyes what I was thinking.

'Because I'm Chinese?'

'I don't know.' It wasn't something I'd ever thought on. Hell, why would you ever ponder on whether Jimmy Stephens would serve a Chinese woman? I guess it depended on what they'd do in old England.

Jimmy, of course, was a gentleman. I do him a disservice to think he'd be anything else. He did a brief double take when he first stood in front of Lin

19

Wu Jia – his mouth opened and closed without him saying anything and his eyes widened – but then he recovered and he smiled with both his mouth and his eyes.

'Welcome to the King's Head,' he said. His accent sounded more English than usual. His smile was warm and inviting. 'What's your pleasure?' I felt a pulse of jealousy – despite the fact that I had only known Lin Wu Jia a matter of seconds.

'Just water, please.' She smiled back at him. Water sounded like *warder*.

'Just water?'

'Yes please.'

If there was a reason not to be welcome in the King's Head – or any of the saloons in St Mary's – it most probably wasn't to be Chinese or female, but to drink just water. Yet Jimmy never even blinked. He picked up a jug off the shelf at the rear of the bar, filled a glass, and presented it to Lin Wu Jia, his eyes crinkling with pleasure.

'Thank you.'

'You're welcome, ma'am,' he said, and from the corner of my eye I saw a few heads turn. Nobody had paid any attention when Lin Wu Jia had entered the bar, but suddenly, with that *ma'am*, she was an object of scrutiny.

'And I'll have another whiskey, Jimmy,' I said.

He nodded, and said to Lin Wu Jia, 'So what brings you here, then? Water aside, of course.'

'Callum Johnson brings me here,' she said,

turning to me, smiling widely as if I alone was worth travelling around the world for. In that moment she looked like a dusty angel.

It was early summer, early afternoon. But it was late so far as drinking time went for most of the men in the King's Head. Some were drunk, some were heading that way, and one or two were already past it. The dry heat that settled in this windless town like a weight riled a few of them and gave others piercing head-aches. Some of the men were weary from life and from lack of good sleep, and others were bored with yet another day in the same place. Some had harridans waiting at home; some had no one. Most of them were here, not in the King's Head, but in St Mary's, because they were either running from something or searching for it. As the day warmed to oven-like temperatures, then patience evaporated, a need for stimulation arose, and a willingness to be cruel for the sake of it awoke within them. Most of all they just wanted to see someone hurt and belittled to make their own painful lives feel not so bad for a few minutes.

'*Ma'am?*' Nash Lane said. 'You finally got yourself a girl, Johnson?'

If there was one man in St Mary's I actively tried to avoid, it was Nash Lane. I had nothing against him, but for as long as I could remember he'd appeared to resent me for something. He was sitting over by the door with Morgan Taylor. Both of them were big guys. Nash Lane made his living doing whatever manual work he could find – be it digging graves, digging footings for buildings, digging irrigation trenches, digging cess pits, building walls or helping put up timber frames. He was married, and Mrs Lane reputedly carried a stick with which she'd hit Nash at every opportunity. The bruises she often sported showed that Nash wasn't averse to hitting her back.

Morgan Taylor had been a marshal at one time, like my father, heading out into the depths of the Territory to bring the bad men back. I don't know what he did these days – some folks say he'd lost his nerve – but one thing he did whenever he could was rile me up about not yet going after Moose Schmidt. A few folk in town knew what I was planning and a couple of them, such as Nash Lane and Morgan Taylor, had started to call me a coward when they needed some minor entertainment to spice up their lives.

Along by the window a couple of other fellows turned to see what was up, grinning when they realized it was me that was the object of Nash Lane's impending attack.

It wasn't that I was disliked, or unpopular. It was simply the fact that I was a kid on the verge of adulthood, a greenhorn. I'd just started drinking in the bars. I was an easy target. Maybe it was the fact that I had my future in front of me, rather than behind, and I occasionally talked about spending that future somewhere other than this place, where these men's future had become their interminable present. It could have been the fact that Samuel Johnson had been my father, and a lot of them had been – still were – jealous of Sam, in awe of him, or just plain scared of him. He had been larger than life. There were even a few men in town who had been brought to justice by Sam Johnson and, having served minor sentences, were back in St Mary's, holding grudges that would never quite fade away. Lastly, and maybe most irritating of all for these men, there was also the fact that there wasn't a prettier woman than my mother in town, and for some reason they held that against me too.

So, since starting frequenting the saloons of St Mary's, I'd had my share of fights. Probably more than my share. I fought my corner best I could. Sam Johnson had taught me well – he'd showed me how a lot of the time cunning and strategy would win a fight just as much as muscles and technique. He also taught me how hesitation and non-commitment would likely lose you a fight. All of which was good, but you still had to practise and learn how to use such ideas in the real world. So I never shied away from confrontation. I was learning, the same as I'd been learning when I drew and shot that Colt over and over up in the woods.

'A girl?' Morgan Taylor said. ' 'Bout time. I heard those mares up at Crawford's ranch get nervous whenever they see you coming.'

Lin Wu Jia looked at me. I couldn't read her

expression. She had the glass of water halfway to her lips. Her hands were steady on the glass and her eyes were steady on me.

'Easy boys,' Jimmy Stephens said. 'It's too hot for trouble. And anyway, the lady's only just arrived.'

'You get Tony and Lowe to buy her and ship her in?' Nash Lane said, looking down the room at Two Bit and Lazy, who were both smiling, happy to be brought into the fray, no doubt looking forward to the ridicule I was about to be made to suffer. 'Like they did for old Avery?'

Now Lin Wu Jia turned and looked over at Nash and Morgan. I could see the muscles around her jawbone start to twitch as she made to say something. But Nash got in first now that he'd had a good look at her.

'A Chinese! You couldn't even afford for them to bring you a white woman?'

'Boys,' Jimmy Stephens said again.

Morgan must have figured that he couldn't let Nash do all the work. He said, 'There's Chinese whores down at the tents. She one of them?' He looked at Jimmy and said, 'You shouldn't let them whores come in the front door, Jimmy. Our wives'll stop us drinking here.'

'She's no whore,' I said. My voice was quiet, but firm. I looked at Lin Wu Jia and then I turned and looked over at Nash Lane.

He grinned back at me. A reaction was what he had wanted. He'd hooked his fish.

'Chinese girl in the Territory,' he said. ' 'Course she's a whore.'

Lin Wu Jia put her hand on my arm.

'She's pretty,' Nash said. 'But don't you get falling for that, Cal. I'm just looking out for you, you know that?'

Lin Wu Jia was turning now. Her coat rode open a little more and I saw she had a gun strapped to her waist. It was only a small gun, but it was a gun nonetheless and I didn't want her drawing it.

'It's OK,' I said to her.

'You got something of your father in you, after all,' Morgan Taylor said. 'He couldn't keep it at home despite your mother being a looker.'

'Perhaps she wasn't giving it to him,' Nash said. 'And he had to find it elsewhere.' The two men laughed.

'Come on, we're going,' I said to Lin Wu Jia.

'You let them say these things?' she said.

'Yeah, you let us say these things?' Nash mocked. 'Tough little Cal who's too scared to ride more'n mile into the Territory. Too scared to do the right thing by his daddy.'

'Or by a Chinese whore,' Morgan said.

'Boys,' Jimmy Stephens said.

'They're just jealous,' I said, pushing myself away from the bar. 'Washed up and jealous, and if what I heard is right even the whores down in Tent City won't let 'em close. The smell, they say.' As soon as I said this, I knew that Nash had won. He'd wanted a reaction and he'd got one. Now he could play the insulted man and the rest would follow the way a blast followed a lit fuse.

'What's that you say, son?' he growled. He scraped his chair backwards and stood up. He was six inches taller than me and a lot heavier. All that digging had given him muscles that a grizzly bear would have been proud of. I'd fought with him a few times before – and lost every time – and knew that if I let him grab me, or even land one of his wild swinging punches, then I probably wouldn't wake up for a week, if at all. In those previous fights there'd always been someone around to pull him off me. Today, looking about the bar, I had the feeling I was on my own.

'Sit down, Nash,' Jimmy Stephens said.

'Hell I will. He accused me of whoring. Him with his own whore right there.'

'He never said that,' Jimmy said. 'Anyway. . . .'

Now Morgan Taylor rose too. His chair fell over and crashed on the floor.

'He accused me of whoring, too,' Morgan said, grinning and trying to look offended at the same time.

I sensed Lin Wu Jia stiffening beside me, maybe getting ready to say something. I didn't want that. She might have been the catalyst for the coming fight, but it would have happened anyway. Maybe if she hadn't been there I could have just walked away – another of my father's lessons was there's always a time when confrontation isn't the right thing. But there's something about a beautiful woman that makes you want to prove yourself. Or do something stupid. Especially at that age.

I took a step away from the bar, towards Nash.

Behind me I heard Dovetail Dave breathe in sharply and say, 'This is going to hurt.'

Nash pushed a table aside and came towards me. Just one table and two chairs remained between us.

'Callum,' Lin Wu Jia said.

'Boys,' Jimmy said behind us. But there was resignation in his voice. I heard him sigh and say, 'You break anything, you pay.'

Nash grabbed one of the chairs by its back and flung it out of the way. His eyes were red-rimmed and there was spittle in the corners of his mouth. His cheeks were flushed beneath his two-day-old stubble, and I could hear his harsh breathing. That was about all that was in my favour – he was overweight and got out of breath just walking to the out-house. Little good that was going to do me in here. But . . .

I circled anti-clockwise around the table towards the swinging doors of the saloon.

*Cunning and strategy.*

He saw what I was doing, but figured the wrong reason.

'You getting ready to run, kid?' he said. 'Folks say you're a coward.'

'Ain't scared of you, Nash,' I lied. Peripheral

vision told me that Morgan was holding back, grinning, happy to let Nash dole out the beating that they both figured I deserved.

Nash snarled like an animal.

I grabbed the last chair that was between us. It felt flimsy and like matchwood in my hand. Nash heaved the table aside and came for me. An oil lamp shattered on the floor and I heard Jimmy Stephens say 'There goes another one,' and then I was swinging that chair at the side of Nash's head.

He lifted his left arm to cushion the blow and simultaneously tried to grab the chair legs. I felt the chair connect with his head and the way the blow jarred up my own arm it must have hurt him. But he acted as if it was nothing. He was drunk on whiskey and filled with adrenaline and rage.

He snatched the chair out of my grip and flung it behind him. His snarl turned into a roar and now he leapt towards me, arms out ready to grab me.

The previous fights with Nash had taught me a little something. Last time out he held me in a bear hug until the final pocket of air had been expelled from my lungs and darkness had started to wash down over my eyes. Doc Mikhailov had smashed a bottle of whiskey on the back of Nash's head that time, and maybe had saved my life. I had no intention of letting Nash do that to me again.

I stepped to the side, rather than away from him. I grabbed his left arm and I pivoted, using his own weight and momentum to swing him around me and towards the batwing doors. There was a moment of surprise in his eyes, then his spine and the back of his head connected with the wooden door frame and the whole building shook. I saw blood spray into the air around the back of his head and then the momentum carried him through the door and onto the plank-walk.

I followed him, running, and I barrelled into him. My shoulder hit him hard in the belly and I heard air burst from his lungs, then he was stumbling backwards, still off balance from my surprise pirouette back in the bar. He hit the ground about a yard out into the street but still managed to hold onto me, his hands grabbing my coat and pulling me towards him, searching for that death grip.

Our faces were inches apart. There was madness in his eyes. His mouth was wide open. He gasped for air and I could smell his stinking breath and see the brown stains on his teeth.

'You . . . sonofabitch,' he tried to say, and I could feel his hands searching for each other behind my shoulders.

I rammed my knee into his stomach. Hard.

Again, it was if the blow was nothing to him.

His hands clasped each other behind my back and I felt myself being pulled closer to his massive frame. I was on top of him, the sun was blazing down and dust was rising up around us. That dust was in my nose, my mouth, my eyes. If he secured his hold and started to squeeze it would be all over.

Maybe for ever.

I twisted, found a few inches leverage, and this time I kneed him in the groin.

His eyes widened and he grimaced and just for a second his hands parted.

I pulled away from his grip, rolled over, and leapt to my feet.

He shook his head as if he couldn't believe what had happened. I should have gone in hard then, kicking him. That's what my father would have done. But instead I played fair. I kept my distance and gave him time to rise. He rolled over onto his arms, spat into the dirt, and gasped harshly for breath.

As he stood up I was aware of people stopping across the street, looking at us, a few moving on, some waiting for the next action. There was a lot of movement behind me, too. Voices and boot-steps as folks rushed out of the King's Head onto the plank-walk.

Nash was still breathing heavily, and he was angrier than hell. He stood for a few seconds, arms hanging, head tilted slightly sideways. He called me some words that would've made the tent-city pimps wince and then he came for me again. But this time he was wise to my tricks and as he reached for me he was ready for my jinking move.

He just wasn't as quick as me.

He got a handful of shirt and nothing else. I heard buttons rip and material tear and then I was free of him.

'You . . . think . . . you're funny?' he said, spitting on the ground again.

We did the same the thing once more, but this time I jinked the other way and he missed me altogether, his back was briefly towards me, and as he rotated to face me I hit him as hard as I could on the mouth.

I may as well have punched a wall.

Now he came again and this time, as I went to move, someone grabbed my arms from behind.

Nash grinned.

I tried to move, twisting and squirming, but Morgan Taylor held me tight. I knew it was Morgan, I could see his arms, his tattered cuffs, and I could hear him breathing right in my ear. He whispered, 'Ain't so good when you can't run, is it?'

I saw Nash forming a fist as big, and no doubt as hard, as a rock. He was grinning. Grinning and dribbling, and his chest was heaving and I saw there was blood in his mouth so I must have hurt him at least a little bit.

He took a step towards me and I just had time to tense my stomach muscles before he ploughed that fist into my belly.

It was like being hit by a lump hammer. The air exploded from my lungs and it felt as if my internal organs had been torn apart. I couldn't breathe. My vision wavered. Pain burst outwards from the centre of my stomach, wave after wave of it. The agony doubled me up, forcing me loose from Morgan Taylor's grip. I was retching and choking, struggling for air, gritting my teeth against the pain. I opened my mouth wide trying to find some oxygen. Then Taylor was gripping me again, straightening me up. It felt like I was being torn in two. I could feel his grip hardening and then my vision cleared and I could see Nash grinning, spittle and blood on his lips. His huge fist forming once more.

But suddenly Taylor's lock on me was gone. His grip just vanished. I vaguely heard a surprised grunt and a hiss of pain, but by then Nash's fist was coming towards me, this time aimed at my face.

I was still in too much pain to react quickly, but I did sway backwards and twist slightly and Nash's punch whistled by my face. He was then off balance because all of that power in his swing hadn't connected with anything.

It was but a split second of opportunity, and I seized it. I punched him on the ear as hard as I could. It may have been imagination but I thought I heard something crack.

The punch hurt my hand. It hurt my belly. But it hurt Nash more. He stumbled in the same direction as the momentum of his punch had pulled him. He tried to catch his balance, but he went down.

I was as mad and as angry as he was now. Morgan Taylor shouldn't have grabbed me like that. I took a step towards Nash intending to kick him, no longer worried about playing fair. He started to rise, made it to all fours, but collapsed again. His hands were splayed out on the dirt and I was on the verge of stamping on one of them, but I saw he was opening and closing his mouth, trying to breathe. There was more blood between his lips. His eyes, when he looked at me, were full of both confusion and pain.

I stepped away from Nash, trying to catch my own breath. I looked around, thinking Morgan Taylor might be coming for me, and could scarcely comprehend what I saw.

Lin Wu Jia was holding Taylor's hand. Actually, it was his fingers. She was holding them in such a way that his hand looked bent backwards, and his arm looked twisted too. It must have been terribly painful for Taylor because whatever Lin Wu Jia was doing – with seemingly no effort – had driven him to his knees. As I watched, she forced him lower and lower and he ended up with his face pressed right into the dirt, pain and curses escaping from his mouth.

I heard gasps of surprise and shock and even nervous laughter from the crowd who had come out of the King's Head. Across the street a couple of people were pointing. Suddenly no one was walking on. They were all stopping and watching.

'Lin Wu . . .,' I said, shaking my head, just about managing to breathe, just about able to cope with the pain still coming from my stomach. I didn't know what else to say.

'Two on one didn't seem fair,' she said, and

smiled. Then she tweaked his fingers again and Morgan Taylor actually screamed.

'We should go,' I said. Nash was still on all fours, shaking his head, dribbling blood.

Lin Wu Jia smiled, made Taylor scream again, then she let go of his fingers and he curled up in a ball; him and Nash Lane both down there in the dirt.

## 4

'Nash Lane?' my mother said. There was something in the way she spoke his name, something in her eyes, which made me want to know more. Especially when she added, 'Yes, I don't think he likes any of us.'

Then she looked across at Lin Wu Jia and said, 'You are very beautiful.'

'Oh no,' Lin Wu Jia said. '*You* are beautiful.'

'What did Callum say your name was?'

'Lin Wu Jia,' I said.

'But please call me Jia,' Lin Wu Jia said. 'It's easier.'

We were in our kitchen, sitting at the table. I'd explained to my ma what had happened, how my clothes had got so torn, and had introduced Jia. I hadn't yet told Ma that it was Jia's mother who Sam Johnson had been working for when he had been killed. That said, my ma was no fool, and I think she had guessed there was a connection.

'Well, Jia,' my mother said. 'Are you hungry? You must have ridden all morning to have got here from anywhere.'

'I'm OK,' Jia said. 'I don't want to put you to any trouble.'

'I'll be making something anyway.'

Jia smiled. 'I might be a little hungry.'

'Then I will make us dinner, and you can tell us all about it.'

'All about what?' I asked, thinking my ma knew something I didn't.

'Whatever it is that brings Jia here,' my mother said.

Jia told us a story.

It had happened just shy of ten years ago at a place called Cape Horn, not far from Sacramento. The Central Pacific Railroad Company was building their end of the line that now stretched across our nation. The Company was literally inching along, sometimes not even making that much progress in a day. They needed to build trestles to span great ravines, blast and drill and chisel out tunnels through rock as hard as iron, and at Cape Horn they had to carve out a ledge on the side of a Sierra Nevada mountain on which the railroad tracks could then be laid.

The Chinese man was known as Yellow Jack, a friendly and jovial man, whose only vice was a little gambling in the end-of-line camp each evening. For this stretch of the construction project, Jack's job was to be lowered down from the clifftop in a wicker basket to bore and fill blast holes in the rock face with a hand-drill.

That September morning there was a sharp chill in the air that cut through Jack's cotton shirt and jacket, but he knew that within a few minutes of starting work he would be sweating, and that he would keep sweating until they hauled him up to the cliff top for dinner.

The drill was heavy, and despite the fact the bit was sharpened every night, it only took a few minutes usage and the edge was gone. Trying to make a hole in the rock felt impossible. He used his chest to press the drill into the rock with as much force as he could, whilst still being able to turn the ratchet. This pressure pushed the basket away from the rock face and meant it was difficult to apply much force anyway. The steel would grind against the rock and within seconds the aged stone would turn white as the bit stripped away the outer surface, but then progress became more difficult, and once there was an indentation about the size of a fingernail it seemed to be a totally futile exercise. Yellow Jack swapped hands often, despite being right-handed. The sweat rolled down his face, back and his flanks. He was hungry, and although he had a water skin with him in the basket it had to last all morning – unless he managed to drill deep enough for a blast before then – so he was careful not to drink too much too soon. He looked at the view often, especially at those moments when he took a rest. The cliff-face stretched back to the west, and all the way along, until the curve of the mountain took them out of sight, he could see fellow countrymen hanging in their own baskets, slowly – so slowly – drilling the rock face. The low morning sun, golden and now warm, cast long horizontal shadows from each hanging man. There were small bushes and plants growing out of the cliff, and way down below, there was a carpet of green – trees that looked soft and inviting from this height. Higher up, snow-covered mountains stretched away in all directions. It was indeed a rare and beautiful sight. The Company paid him, too. He reminded himself of this fact whenever the pain in his hands and in his chest became too much. It was better than trying to make a living back home – especially with the Taiping army on the rampage. So he pressed against the rock and he forced the drill to grind around and around, gaining tiny fractions of an inch every few minutes.

At lunchtime, his nephew, Liu, and another man, Chen, hauled Yellow Jack up to the top. Liu and Chen ran six ropes. The ropes were a hundred yards apart and Liu and Chen's job was to lower the men, pull them up at lunchtime or whenever they were ready to initiate a blast, then lower them back down as required. Liu always kept some rice and fish cooking, and every few minutes he would run between each rope to make sure the men doing the drilling were OK. Chen, who was older than Liu, sat in the sun and waited for Liu to call him whenever he needed some assistance.

The eight men – the six drillers, Liu and Chen – gathered around Liu's cooking pot and helped themselves to food. There was a bottle of wine and the men poured a little into tin cups. They lay down and closed their eyes. There was a cold wind up there on the top and it dried the sweat from the men's clothes and from their skin. Yellow Jack fooled absent-mindedly with two ivory dice that he always carried with him. But it only felt like a couple of minutes before the Company man was yelling at them from a hundred yards away that it was time to get back to it. The men groaned – especially Liu who was only small, and now had the job to lower each man in turn. He, Chen and the driller who had been first up, wandered back along the cliff-top to the man's basket. Liu asked him, as he would each man in turn, how soon he'd need lifting up out of the way of a blast. Within thirty minutes all six men were back down at the cliff-face, hanging in their baskets, drilling the rock.

Each basket rope was attached to a tree way behind them on the cliff-top. It was also wrapped around several deep iron spikes that had been driven into the ground with lump-hammers. At the cliff edge was an iron frame holding a wheel. The rope ran around the grooved wheel. Like the iron spikes, the edge-frame had been driven into the ground. Sometimes these frames popped loose, but so long as the spikes and the rope around the tree held – which they did most of the time – then the suspended baskets were reasonably safe.

About two o'clock in the afternoon, one of the men some four hundred yards back from Yellow Jack called up to Liu that he was ready to blast. Liu waited until the man gave him the nod that he'd lit the long fuse and then Liu and Chen hauled the man up, hand over hand, heaving the basket and its occupant to safety.

Along the cliff-face the men still hanging paused from their drilling, held their breath, and looked back towards where the blast was expected. Usually a puff of smoke was the first thing they saw, then came a rumbling sound and sometimes – depending on the density of the rock – the loud crack of the explosion. After that the shattered rock burst outwards, a big cloud of dust and shale and stone that filled the air and seemed to float for a whole minute or more. Once, a bird flying by had been hit – and most probably killed – by a stone no bigger than a bullet and the men had cheered as if someone had pulled off a miracle gunshot.

Then it was back to work until the next blast.

Yellow Jack was ready to blast around four o'clock that afternoon. His shadow was now on the opposite side of the cliff-face to where it had been in the morning. His chest and shoulders ached. His hands and arms felt as heavy as lead. The hole he'd bored went deep in the rock and he laid his drill down on the woven floor of the basket, and pulled out several black powder cartridge rolls from a small leather bag. He pushed the cartridges deep into the hole, slowly ramming them in with a flat-ended iron rod. Into the last cartridge he inserted a long fuse. He pushed this into the cliff-face too, and then he sealed the hole with rock-paste – a concoction made up of stone dust, sand and cement powder, that he poured a little of his water into. It dried quickly and he pressed it into the hole, then added more.

He looked up, following the line of his rope to the top of the cliff where white clouds were starting to fill the cold blue sky.

'Liu! Liu!'

He called a few times before his nephew appeared at the top. There was no hurry. The longer the plug had to dry the better the blast.

'I'm ready,' he said. 'Is Chen there with you?'

'Yes. We're ready too.'

'I'm OK to light the fuse?'

'Yes.'

Yellow Jack took a box of Lucifers from his pocket, scratched one into life, and held it against the end of the fuse, which spluttered, sizzled, and sparked like a string of rabbit fat dripping into a fire.

He looked up at the cliff-top, but Liu was gone. He'd be standing a few yards back, his leather gloves on, him and Chen getting ready to heave that basket up.

'Pull!' Yellow Jack shouted. 'It's lit! Pull!'

Liu wasn't sure if he had seen the man around before. The man might have gambled with them once or twice in the evenings, but Liu wasn't sure of that either. White men tended to look alike to him, and anyway the Americans didn't mix with the Chinese. When the man came closer Liu felt a rising sense of unease. He wasn't sure why. The man had been hanging around for a while over by the trees. He seemed to be checking knots. For a crazy moment Liu had wondered if the man was loosening rather than checking the ropes.

When Jack had shouted up that he was ready for a blast Liu had been standing a few baskets along. It was too late in the afternoon to run, so he walked slowly back along the cliff-top, slipping his gloves on as he came, and by the time he got to Jack's rope the man was there, too.

'All OK, sir?' he said to the man. Chen was there, as well, putting on his gloves.

The man smiled. He had bright blue eyes. 'Carry on.'

Liu looked over the edge of the cliff and Jack was down there, looking up.

'I'm ready,' Jack said.

Liu said, 'We're ready, too.'

Jack asked if it was OK to light the fuse and Liu

said yes, still looking over the edge. He saw Jack flick a match into life, and then Liu turned to go and grab the rope. He vaguely heard Jack say, 'It's lit! Pull me up!'

Sometimes something is so out of place, so out of the ordinary, that it takes a moment to comprehend it.

Chen was lying on the ground, his eyes wide open in fear – or maybe surprise – and his throat was gaping wide open like another mouth. Blood was pouring all down his shirt and there was a wheezing sound coming from his sliced windpipe.

There was a revolver in the man's hand pointing at Liu.

'Don't move,' the man said.

Liu half-raised his hands. He looked around. The cliff-top was deserted. The set of ropes he was in charge of stretched for almost half a mile.

'I have to pull him up,' Liu said. 'He's lit the fuse.'

He tore his eyes from the man and looked at Chen. Chen was now lying still. The blood was no longer pulsing from the wound as if it was being pumped from somewhere, but it was still running over the jagged edges of the flesh and soaking his shirt, his jacket, the grass where he lay.

Liu looked back at the man.

'I have to pull him up!'

As if on cue Jack's voice rose from below. 'Pull me up, Liu! The fuse is lit.'

Liu lowered his hands and went to grab the rope. 'Don't move!'

The man thrust the revolver forward. Liu was close enough that he could see the dark silver bullets in the cylinder.

'Liu!' Jack called. There was panic in his voice.

The man shook his head.


Yellow Jack snatched at the burning fuse, trying to smother it with his hands. He had gloves in the basket but there wasn't time to put them on. The fuse burned the palms of his hands. He cried out in pain and yanked his scorched hands away. The fuse kept on sizzling. He yelled out to Liu again. If his nephew was playing a joke then it wasn't funny. Jack would kick him all around the camp later. But no, Liu would never make a joke this way. Jack tried again to grab the fuse and yank it out of the hole, out of the cemented plug he had so carefully and solidly wedged into the rock. But his burned hands were too tender to get a good grip and they slipped on the fuse. When he tried reaching out to the rock face with one hand for leverage the movement pushed the basket away from the cliff.

From the corner of his eye he saw Daway Ma in the next basket, a hundred yards away, pointing at him, waving furiously.

Again he grabbed the fuse, pulling it as hard as the pain would allow, and now he felt it move slightly. But it was impossible to hold onto the fire and he couldn't help but let go. The fuse lay hanging against the cliff face, still smouldering, the sparks right up to the cement plug now.

'Liu!' he called.

But it was too late. Even if his nephew started pulling him up now he'd get caught in the blast.

Jack gritted his teeth. He thought back to the days as a young man when the monks trained him in fighting and in overcoming pain. He reached out and grabbed the fuse and this time he held it as tight as he could, ignoring the agony searing outwards from his burnt hands, and he pulled with all his might.

The cement plug came loose and the fuse broke free from the black powder cartridge inside the hole.

He fell back into the basket, not caring about the way the sudden movement made the basket swing precariously. He closed his eyes. He breathed a long sigh of relief. Tears came.

The man said, 'Wait.'

Liu's breath came in short gasps, first through his mouth, then his nose. His hands were shaking and his shoulders and neck were tense, readying themselves for an explosion.

Chen's dead eyes were looking right at him. It was strange how you could know that a man was dead by just looking at his eyes, even if they appeared no different to how they had been when he was living.

'Please . . .' Liu said.

'Wait.'

Now they heard Jack shouting up again. 'Pull me up, Liu. What's going on?'

Liu looked at the man. The urgency had gone out of Jack's voice and the man had noticed it.

'Don't move,' the man said.

He circled around Liu, keeping the revolver aimed at the young rope man. When he got close to the edge of the cliff the man peered over.

Liu heard Jack saying, 'Liu . . . Who are you?' Liu tensed himself, ready to spring at the man, maybe knock him over the cliff. But the man turned.

'He pulled the fuse out,' the man said, and shot Liu. The bullet hit Liu in the chest and knocked him backwards. The man walked towards Liu, levering back the hammer on his revolver. He looked down at Liu, seemingly studying Liu's shocked eyes. The man smiled. Then he shot Liu a second time.

'What's going on?' Jack called from the basket hanging hundreds of feet over the green canopy that had looked so soft and inviting from such a height.

The man sighed. He turned the cylinder of his revolver so that the hammer rested on one of the empty chambers and he slipped the revolver back in his holster. Then he walked over to Liu's fire where there was still a pot of rice and fish bubbling. The man picked up three burning sticks from the edge of the fire and carried them over to the rope that held up Jack's basket. He made a little tripod of the burning sticks beneath the rope and watched as the flames flickered in the breeze, appeared to die, and then caught again. The man saw how the flames started to blacken the rope, and he waited until the rope itself started to burn. He watched a while longer.

Then he grinned and walked away.

'Liu was my cousin,' Jia said. There were tears in her eyes, but not so many that they spilled over onto her cheeks. I could tell it was a story that she had told, or at least experienced many times. She looked at my mother and then she looked at me. 'Jack was my father,' she said.

'And the man?' I asked, although I already knew the answer.

'The man was Moose Schmidt,' Jia said.

**5**

We'd finished dinner but we still sat at the kitchen table. I asked Jia how they had known the man who had killed her father and her cousin had been Schmidt.

Jia told how her father had still been alive when rescuers found him, broken and tangled amongst the rocks and trees at the base of the cliff. Before he died, he described the man that had been looking over the cliff edge. Daway Ma, who had been in the next basket along had seen him, too. Other men told how Moose Schmidt had been working in the camp, but he disappeared after that incident. And later, in his early travels across the Territory, Schmidt boasted about the killings, too.

'And me?' I said. 'How . . . Why?'

'My mother,' Jia said. 'You met her.'

'Yes.'

'She told me that your father was the only one who ever came close to killing Moose Schmidt.'

My mother said, 'Sam would still be alive if all he'd had to do was kill that man. I believe your mother wanted Schmidt alive.'

'Yes. That is true. But now . . . Me . . . I just want him dead.'

'Me, too,' I said.

My mother stood up and put a pot of water on the stove in the corner, her back to Jia and I. She hated the idea of my going after Schmidt, but had long been resigned to the fact that one day it would happen. It wasn't that she didn't have faith in me, but she knew – more than I did – just how evil, resilient and slippery Schmidt was. To my mother the whole thing felt pre-ordained, like one of those ancient Greek tragedies. I could see it in her eyes some days that she thought she had already lost me, but that it just hadn't happened yet.

Jia said, 'That's why I came. I know you want to go after him, too.'

'How did you know?'

'There's talk.'

My mother turned and looked at me. She didn't need to say anything. I knew what she was thinking, and she I. If there was talk about my intentions and Jia had heard such talk, what were the odds that Moose Schmidt had heard it too? Not that I was going to shoot Schmidt in the back, but a certain amount of surprise would have been a good thing.

'Together,' Jia said. 'We will succeed.'

'You wear a gun,' I said. 'And that thing you did

to Morgan Taylor. . . .'

I was intrigued about Jia's capabilities, but I was also keen to reassure my mother that together Jia and I might indeed succeed.

Before Jia could answer, the street door opened, and a moment later the kitchen door.

Amos Bowler was one of my mother's boarders – at the moment her only boarder. A short man who always wore a blue suit and a bowler hat. I don't know what his surname really was, I just called him Bowler because of that hat. His cheeks were red as if he had been hurrying, or drinking. Or both.

'Oh you're here,' he said, looking at Jia and I.

'Good evening, Amos,' my mother said. I said hello, too. Then I introduced Jia who stood up and did that little bow from the shoulders again.

'I heard about you,' Amos said, smiling at Jia. Then he turned and addressed my mother.

'Nash Lane and Morgan Taylor. . . .'

'I know,' my mother said.

'You know what?'

'I know what happened.'

Now Amos looked at me. 'He's coming after you. Nash Lane, I mean.'

'I guessed he wouldn't be able to leave it.'

'Soon as he can stand up,' Amos said.

'Can't he stand up?'

'He keeps falling over. You did something to his balance, by all accounts.'

'It's probably drink,' my mother said. I could

hear the water starting to bubble on the stove.

'No. They say he sobered up quick enough after the fight,' Amos said. 'But he can't walk more'n two steps without needing to hold on to something.' He looked at me again. 'He's really mad. I mean, really.'

'He initiated the trouble,' Jia said.

'Don't doubt that,' Amos said. He looked at Jia and pulled a face as if he didn't really want to say what he was about to. 'Morgan Taylor ain't happy either. I wouldn't be surprised if Nash doesn't come after Cal with a gun. But Morgan Taylor says he has other plans for you.' Amos's uncomfortable expression grew a little more strained. 'He says you're a Chinese whore and there's only one sort of thing a whore understands.'

Jia blushed a little. Maybe it was anger.

'He can try,' she said. I don't think she knew she was doing it, but her hand moved as she spoke and rested on the gun that she still had strapped to her waist.

'They've got friends,' Amos said. 'My advice would be to lay very low for a while.'

For a moment the kitchen was silent, then my mother said, 'Who would like coffee?'

When I had been younger and my father had spent time at home there was a place he used to take me – and sometimes my mother, too – for an overnight camp. It wasn't that far from St Mary's Gap, just a couple of hours ride, but it was far enough for it to be an adventure for a young boy.

It was a tiny settlement that had long been abandoned in a hollow with trees and hills surrounding it. A creek flowed not far from the edge of the settlement. My father said it had been a surveyor's camp that had one time been in the middle of nowhere. There were several log cabins – and the fact they were all aligned nicely in a square and the walls were straight and the roofs solid and they had windows did suggest surveyors, or at least some group of people with attention to detail and pride in their workmanship. There was a privy built over a deep drop hole, and a hundred yard trench that had been dug to divert the creek. In one of the log cabins there was still a pile of tangled rusting chains – not normal chains, but chains with long straight links. Surveyor's chains. There were some old picks and spades, too. Rabbits had colonised the place and the shooting – and eating – was good. They were fun times, if infrequent and few.

Jia and I collected our horses from the livery midevening and around two in the morning we prepared to slip quietly out of St Mary's Gap and head towards that camp.

My mother hugged me, and after a slight pause as if neither she nor Jia quite knew the etiquette, she hugged Jia too.

I told Ma that we wouldn't be long and she gave me that look again, the one that tried to instil belief in me and in herself, whilst still feeling the weight of fate bearing down upon us.

I asked her about Nash Lane. What would she do or say, if – when – he came around.

'Don't worry about Nash,' she said. 'I can handle him. I've been handling him for years.'

Then Jia and I rode out beneath the soft moonlight, with one intent: to kill a man.

**6**

When we were far enough clear of St Mary's that our voices wouldn't carry on the cold night air I asked Jia what had happened with her mother. The story I'd heard was that Moose Schmidt had shot her in the back. Was this true?

'Yes, it's true,' Jia said. 'My mother's name was Yu Yan. It means beautiful smile. My mother was very beautiful.'

'I know.'

'We lived in a province of China where the war was bad and my father and my uncle and a few others took us away. We travelled long time and eventually we made it to London where there were other Chinese. We were happy there and we should have stayed but we were poor and it was a hard life. Stories came in about gold in America and many of the men decided to go. They would send for us when they had made their fortune – and they did indeed send money and we thought it was only a matter of time.'

'He ended up working on the railroad,' I said.

'Yes. When the money stopped we were puzzled for many months and then a letter arrived and we knew what had happened. Many men died in accidents, but this was murder.'

She added, 'In our culture such a thing has to be avenged.'

'In any culture.'

'Yes.'

We let the horses find their own way and set their own pace as we rode north. I looked across at Jia, but in the darkness I couldn't see her face. To our right there was already a little blue light in the sky, but it only served to make Jia – who was riding on that side of me – even darker.

'My mother was what we in China call, *Wu*.'

'*Wu?*'

'Yes. Here you would call her . . . I don't know. Maybe a witch.'

'Your mother was a witch?'

'Yes. Well, no. It's not the same thing. *Wu* is good. *Ku* is the bad side. My mother was *Wu*. She could heal people. She was good with needles.'

I looked at Jia's silhouette against the lightening sky. It had always been hard to understand the Indians out here in the Territory. Their world, their beliefs, their behaviours seemed impossible to comprehend sometimes. Now here was someone from the other side of the world bringing more confusion into my life. For a moment I felt very small, very insignificant, and very ignorant.

'Needles?' I said.

'I will show you if the need arises.'

'You are *Wu*, too?'

'A little. But I followed my father more.'

'And what was he?'

'He was a fighter.'

A witch and a fighter. I smiled in the darkness. Moose Schmidt might have a surprise coming yet.

Jia said, 'We were too far away for my mother to be able to make a difference, so we came to America, too. New York.'

'And from there your mother went to Natchez,' I said.

'Yes. But this all took a long time. From New York my mother arranged for some men to find Moose Schmidt. It was from one of them that your father's name came up.'

'My father was known in New York?'

'The man sent a message to New York with your father's name. He told my mother that Moose was too elusive. Maybe even too terrible. He said no one could bring him back alive. The man said something like: well, maybe Sam Johnson could. And that's when my mother came to find your father.'

'If only she'd wanted Moose dead.'

'Yes. But she wanted to be the one.'

'To kill him?'

'Yes.'

I thought of that beautiful and exotic woman my father and I had met on the banks of the Mississippi. It was hard to believe that she would have been able to kill anyone, let alone actually want to.

'After your father, she tried a few more men, but no one could catch Moose Schmidt. He was like a demon, or a ghost, my mother said. One day she woke and she said she'd had a vision, or a dream, and that she saw what had to happen. She had to go after Moose Schmidt herself.'

'She went herself, despite all of the men failing?'

'She'd seen herself killing him in the vision. She wasn't scared.'

'And what happened?'

'In her letters she told how she had got close to him. It wasn't long ago. It was late last year just before the snow. He was living in a town called Three Oaks. My mother arrived in the town and contrived to meet him, look at him, and make eye contact. After that, she made sure she met him often. He was uneasy about her – although I don't think he knew why. If he ever spoke about killing my father, he did so dismissively. I mean, he didn't speak to my mother on the subject. My mother once asked someone else to question him about it, and he said, "Those Chinamen? That was nothing. There were thousands of them. What was two? Hell, you want to come after me for a killing come after me for something worthwhile.'"

The first rays of the sun were stretching up over the eastern horizon now. Jia's face was golden in the low light. She was looking straight ahead. Her profile was strong and proud and she was so pretty I could have stared at her for a long time.

The abandoned settlement wasn't far now. If I remembered rightly it was just over the next rise. The idea was to sleep a while, on account of we'd had no rest this night, and then formulate a plan. I'd said we should go towards Green Springs because that's where One Leg Hawk was. One Leg had always been a good source of news about Schmidt. I think he wanted to kill Schmidt as much as I did and as much as Jia did. So Green Springs was the plan. But in the light of what Jia had said, Three Oaks was an option, too.

'My mother's wanted to get Moose alone,' Jia said.

'Brave woman.'

'She was. She quickly built a reputation helping people with pain. You know, the needles?'

'The needles,' I said.

'She supposed a man who had lived the life that Moose had lived must have some pains that wouldn't go away and she asked someone, maybe the same man who had asked Moose about the killings, to mention my mother to him, to say how she could help him. My mother could make pain vanish.'

I wanted to ask, was Yu Yan going to kill Moose

with needles? But I refrained. It wasn't a night for joking.

Jia said, 'Moose was apparently open to the idea. He did have a bad limp from a wound that had never healed properly and gave him much trouble. But something spooked him. I think he went to visit my mother and he saw something in her eyes. If we have a weakness in our family,' Jia said, and she looked across at me and her face was again in darkness, although I knew the rising sun was illuminating my face now, 'it's that our eyes give too much away. I don't know what happened inside his head – maybe he started thinking about the killing of those Chinese men all that time ago – but a few days later he shot my mother in the back.'

'There were witnesses? I mean, people know it was him?'

'I know it was him,' she said. 'He killed my father, and he killed my mother. I'm the last one standing now.'

'I'm here, too,' I said.

'Yes. Yes, you are.'

A ray of sunlight caught her smile. In the quarter light of such an early dawn I could see that it was a sad smile.

We slept in a dry hut, warm under our blankets, and in the late morning when we woke I made a fire and I started cooking meat and potatoes. When Jia came outside, she brewed tea from leaves that she had brought with her.

'I was going to cook you a rice breakfast,' she said, tasting the food I had made. 'But this is good. Thank you.'

'Rice?'

'I have some with me. Rice, ginger, dried fish. You might like it.'

We looked around the camp and I explained how once upon a time this had been a wilderness, a frontier, and back then no one had known what lay beyond. I told her stories of my camping trips with my father and my mother and she said, 'I like your mother. She's beautiful. But she's strong, too.' Then she smiled, and said, 'I see her in you.'

I think I might have blushed.

I was still young enough and, I suppose, shy enough around women that I needed to divert the subject away from my own attributes, so I quickly asked Jia about her gun. She looked at me and I knew she understood exactly why I was manoeuvring the conversation in another direction. She smiled, her eyes crinkled mischievously, and I wondered about all that life experience she had recounted and how it gave her a confidence that I liked. I liked a lot.

She slipped the revolver from her holster and handed it to me. It was smaller than my own Army Colt.

'I was given it in London,' she said. 'I believe it was made there.'

'Five shots,' I said.

'Yes.'

'And they're all empty?'

She smiled and shrugged. 'I have powder and balls in my saddle-bag. . . .'

'With the rice,' I said.

'Yes, with the rice. But I don't fire the gun very often and my uncle, who gave me the gun, said that the powder would get damp if I loaded it and didn't use it. It was damper in London than it is here.'

The gun had a lovely blue finish to the metal and a walnut grip. I lifted it and, despite it being empty, pointed it away from us. It was something my father had always been insistent on. I squeezed the trigger and was surprised to find it was a double-action, albeit a stiff double-action.

'That's nice,' I said. Mine was one of the older single-action types. 'Are you good with it?'

'No, not really. It's hard to pull. But it's reassuring to have.'

'Yes. A gun always is.' I gave her the revolver back and she looked at it with a bit more interest than she had shown prior to handing it to me. 'It's amazing to think it comes from London, from halfway round the world.'

'That means I come from all the way around the world.'

'And that's amazing, too,' I said, and we looked at one another and we both smiled.

Later we talked about what we knew of Moose

Schmidt and we agreed we would head towards Green Springs, and One Leg Hawk.

Everything considered, it was as good a place as any to start.

# 7

I had travelled to see One Leg Hawk a few times over the years, although not for a while, so I knew his house. It was a two-room pinewood cabin standing alone on the outskirts of Green Springs. Although these days, we discovered, the cabin was no longer on the outskirts. But it still stood alone, plenty of empty ground all around and a clear view of the sky and the distant hills, which is how One Leg liked it.

We pulled the horses to a halt outside the house.

A girl I hadn't seen before appeared from around the side of the cabin, a broom in her hand. 'He's not here,' she said. She was an Indian girl with a hard, weather-lined face, but she was young – maybe twenty years old. She had black hair with two long braids and she wore a green dress. She was barefoot and had a leather belt tied around the green dress. There was a knife in a scabbard on the belt.

'He still live here?' I asked.

'Yes.'

'One Leg Hawk?' I said, just to make sure we were talking about the same man.

'Yes. *Tawodi*.' I'd never heard it before but I guessed that was One Leg's Cherokee name.

'Where is he?' Jia asked. The girl didn't appear to be about to proffer any information of her own accord.

'Out back of the Silver Spur. You'll find him there. They're fighting roosters.'

We rode deeper into Green Springs, watered the horses at the troughs in the centre, and then found the Silver Spur. It was a one-storey saloon with a high false front, painted in bright colours that had faded in the sun. Several horses were roped to the hitching rail out front. From the back we could hear the sound of people shouting and swearing, laughing, and then swearing some more.

For a moment I thought about asking – suggesting – that Jia wait for me with the horses whilst I went to find One Leg. But she was already dismounting, and if I'd learned one thing in the few hours that I'd known her it was that she wasn't one for avoiding anything or adhering to anyone else's expectations of a young Chinese woman.

Together we walked along the side of the Silver Spur and into the yard at the rear.

There must have been thirty or forty men there, and a handful of women. No one noticed Jia and I. They were all crowded around a make-shift pit – a rough square about twelve feet on each side made with planks of timber roped and wired together and resting against barrels at each corner. There were two fighting birds within the pit, and at opposite corners, two men, both crouched down, both yelling instructions, clapping their hands, and whistling in a strange staccato style. The men looked like farmers, as did many in the crowd, but I noticed a few of the onlookers wore guns. Others, I assumed, were range-hands, some even appeared to be businessmen. There were several Indians. A couple of the women looked like saloon girls. All of them let out *ohhs* and *ahhs* in unison as the birds struck out at each other. People shrieked and gasped. Some laughed, but it was that uncomfortable laugh that hides fear. One man, in a bowler hat much like my mother's boarder Amos, clutched a sheaf of paper money and was shouting about there still being time to bet, that ladies and gentlemen, it wasn't too late.

The air reeked of sweat and smoke and of the Silver Spur outhouse that was over on the far side of the yard. I could hear the high-pitched nervous sound of gamecocks, not the two that were fighting, but of others that were caged around the edge of the clearing. Alongside the cages, lying in the dirt, I could see the blood-stained carcass of a dead cock.

I don't know if I did it for her or for me, and even why, but I reached out and held Jia's hand. She didn't resist.

I could see One Leg Hawk on the far side of the pit. He was wearing a blue felt hat and his black hair was long and braided like the girl's hair back at his cabin. He was wearing a dirty tan jacket and he looked older than I remembered, his skin lined and weathered and tight against his prominent cheek bones.

He must have sensed something, for he tore his gaze away from the pit and he looked directly at me. It took a moment for recognition to occur then his dark sunken eyes widened, his mouth opened, and turned into a smile. He nodded and then, pulled by events in the cock-pit, he looked away from me and back at the fight. Happy he wasn't missing anything, he again looked at us. I pointed to myself and then at him to indicate we'd come round to where he was, and then, still holding Jia's hand we edged along behind the crowd.

It was impossible not to look at the fight.

The cocks were white, or had been before the contest. They were now blood-stained. They both had red feathers standing proud around their heads and fans of black feathers at the tail. There were white, red, and black feathers strewn on the dirt, and as we watched the birds suddenly leapt upwards, thrashing and kicking and swiping at one another. There was a spray of blood in the air. The birds were making strange cries, as if they didn't have enough energy or oxygen for a full-blown scream or shriek. Though they looked similar in colour, one bird, the one closest to One Leg, was smaller than the other. The thought crossed my mind that it wasn't a fair fight, that with all those other gamecocks in the cages then surely a fairer match-up could have been made. As if it was reading my mind, the bigger bird suddenly rushed forward on the ground, kicking out, and I saw the long silver spike that had been bound to its leg with red twine. The smaller bird thrashed its wings and rose a few inches, just enough to avoid the flashing blade. This time it did find enough energy to scream and I felt myself wince at the fear in the creature's cry.

The bigger bird moved in as the smaller one landed. The smaller one had a silver spike attached to its leg, too. As the big bird came towards it, now jabbing with its beak towards the other's eyes, the small bird rose up again and kicked out. But the larger bird parried the attack by rushing in close, and effectively stopping the leg movement of the small bird. Big bird thrust its beak towards small one's eyes again. There was more shrieking, more blood mist, a flurry of feathers were torn loose.

Then the little bird rolled over, twisted back and forth like a dog or an eel trying to get loose from an unwanted grip, flapped its wings and suddenly put a few feet between it and the big bird. There was a growing bloodstain on the little bird's breast and it was shaking its head as if it was struggling to breathe.

A bell rang, and with it came instant groans and complaints.

'General was about to win!' someone yelled.

'You can't stop it now.'

'Cheat!!'

A man on the outside far corner of the pit, just along from One Leg, said, 'Rules is rules. That was eight minutes. Two minutes rest.'

There were more mutterings, but it seemed to me there was a general acceptance of the situation. *Rules is rules.* And, anyway, I couldn't see that two minutes rest was going to make any difference to the eventual outcome.

Jia and I walked along the far side of the pit towards One Leg. I noticed the owner of the small bird was blowing down its beak.

'Clearing the blood from its throat,' Jia said.

I looked at her in amazement. She smiled at me.

We reached One Leg.

He smiled and nodded as if accepting that something he had long anticipated was finally happening. I held out my hand and he took it in both his and grasped it without actually shaking it.

'Young Cal,' he said.

'One Leg Hawk. It's good to see you.'

He stared at me, not blinking, still smiling. His eyes had a yellow tinge to them, his teeth too. This close his skin looked as tough – and the same colour – as my horse saddle. He smelled of tobacco and whiskey.

'It's good to see you, too,' he said.

'This is Jia,' I said, realizing I was still holding her hand.

One Leg Hawk tore his eyes from mine and he looked at her and his smile widened.

'Please to meet you, Jia,' he said. 'A pretty name for a pretty girl.'

She smiled and did her little bow and told him that she was pleased to meet him, too.

'One minute!' the man with the bell yelled.

'Still time for a wager,' the bowler-hatted man called out. 'Good odds on Rattle. I'll tell you what – *excellent* odds on Rattle! Five to one!!' A few people laughed. Rattle's owner had a cloth out now and was wiping the blood from his bird's eyes.

'Rattle is the little bird?' Jia said, looking at One Leg.

'Yes,' he said.

'Like a rattlesnake,' she said.

'Not today. General's too strong.'

'No,' Jia said. 'Rattle is thinking. General is not.'

One Leg looked at her, furrows of puzzlement appearing on his forehead.

'General is just plunging forward. He's getting tired. Rattle is quick – like the snake he's named after.'

'Rattle will win?' One Leg asked.

'After two minutes rest? Yes,' Jia said. There was no doubt in her voice. 'Rattle will win. It won't take long.'

One Leg stared at her for a few seconds. There appeared to be an exchange between them, not words, or even knowledge, just faith, I guess.

'Hold on,' One Leg said, and he turned away from us and he shouted across to the man in the bowler hat. 'Reuben! Hey Rube. I will have ten dollar on Rattle! Rube! Five to one!'

Rube looked at One Leg and nodded. A few people laughed. A few more looked over and grinned and shook their heads at the stupidity of some people.

The bell went.

One Leg said to Jia, 'You're sure?'

Jia smiled.

This time, when the two handlers released their birds, the gamecocks stood for a few seconds, very still, eyes locked on one another. Their heads and bodies and tails were parallel to the floor, not the upright stand of a rooster in the yard, but a flat, fighting stance. Both blood-stained chests were heaving as if two minutes rest hadn't been long enough. One of them cried out, a sound as if dawn was approaching, and the other's head twitched, but still they didn't move. I wondered if they understood any of what they were being made to do, or if it was all instinct. For a few seconds neither looked keen to recommence combat. The onlookers were quiet, too. It wasn't total silence, I could hear harsh breathing and some whispered words, the rustle of clothing, the scratch of a Lucifer. I could smell pipe tobacco and whiskey, cheap perfume and unwashed clothes. I felt the temperature of the whole yard seemingly rising. For those few seconds, anticipation was everything.

Then General lunged forwards and suddenly both roosters flew upwards in a blurred tangle of slashing feet. The sunlight flashed off a silver spike and one of the cocks squealed. Around the makeshift pit the onlookers burst into life, shouting encouragement, yelling out tactics as if the birds could understand them.

The birds landed and paused again, once more staring at each other, struggling for breath. They no longer had the fierce energy they had been displaying when Jia and I had first arrived a few minutes earlier. I heard One Leg whispering something to himself. He cast a quick look at me, and then at Jia. She smiled and nodded, and One Leg nodded back.

General lunged again, wings thrashing at the hot dusty air. He rose two feet and Rattle appeared to struggle to get to the same height, but again their legs and claws and the attached sharpened spikes were just a blur. Three, four times, the pattern was repeated, a pause for breath, the eye-balling, then one of the birds lunging forwards and upwards, a few seconds shrieking and effort, blood and feathers in the air, the crowd getting louder. Over and over. Smoke hung all around the cockpit now from

71

the cigarettes. Dust motes shone like tiny particles of suspended silver in the sunlight.

Then, after a particular vicious coupling in mid-air, General came down not on his feet, but on his side. Where he landed the dirt was immediately soaked in blood. In a flash Rattle was upon his opponent, thrashing and stabbing in a series of lightning fast movements that looked random, but must have had very specific intent. I heard someone say '*heart-shot*' and General somehow scrabbled backwards, away from his assailant. General's breast was bright crimson, no white left in the feathers at all, and his eyes were wide and full of fear. He sat flat to the dirt, no longer moving his body, just his eyes darting around, looking at Rattle, unable now to defend itself.

Rattle's handler stepped forward quickly and grabbed his bird before it could do any more damage. He kissed it and held aloft, grinning, and I saw the owner had very few teeth. A few people cheered, but more groaned. The other handler picked General up. He was gentle and he held the bird close to his own chest, the bird's blood making his dark blue shirt even darker. I watched him looking at General and I saw him shaking his head. Then I heard One Leg Hawk calling out to Reuben. 'Rube! It's payday, Rube!'

I discovered I had been holding my breath.

A minute or two later, as he was stuffing his winnings into an inside pocket, One Leg Hawk turned to me, his expression serious, and said, 'So it's time, is it?'

I nodded.

One Leg said, 'Come inside. Let me buy you a drink. We will talk.'

We went into the Silver Spur. I noticed how badly One Leg limped as he walked. The saloon was very quiet on account of most of the patrons were out the back preparing for the next fight. We could still hear them shouting and talking, laughing and cursing, still hear Reuben yelling odds. We sat at a small round table by the window. One Leg drank whiskey, I drank whiskey and water, and Jia drank water on its own.

'You know birds?' One Leg asked Jia.

She took a long draught of water. 'There was a lot of fighting where I come from. Birds and otherwise.'

'And you saw something in Rattle?'

'People most usually see what they want to see,' she said. 'And most don't look beyond the big fighter. The longer the fight went on, the better the little bird's chances. The big one was already tired when we arrived.'

One Leg nodded, then he lifted his whiskey glass and saluted her.

He turned to me. 'I feared, but I also hoped, this day would come.'

'The time is right,' I said.

He looked again at Jia. He drank some more

whiskey and he said, 'Moose Schmidt shot a Chinese lady in the back in Three Oaks.'

'My mother,' Jia said.

He looked at me. '*Your* father, *her* mother.'

I said, 'Her father, too. Many years ago. On the railroad.'

One Leg started to roll himself a cigarette.

'He's a very bad man. A monster, it is said.'

'He murdered Jia's cousin, too.'

'And many more,' One Leg said. 'He gave me this limp. I don't understand it but the doctor says the bullet wound in my chest gives me a limp in the leg. Some days I can hardly walk. Can't ride a horse no more. Haven't been able to in a long time. But I guess I was lucky.'

'Who's the girl at your house?' I asked. 'You have a daughter?'

He grinned. 'I have a wife. It's only my leg that is limp.'

I thought I saw Jia blush. She lifted her glass of water and sipped gently.

'I will take you to meet her,' One Leg said. 'First, let's have another drink.'

'And you know where Moose Schmidt is?' I asked.

'Yes,' he said. 'I know where Moose Schmidt is.'

## 8

One Leg Hawk lay naked on his kitchen table. He was face-down on a blanket. A square of folded cloth covered his rump. Evening sunlight, coming through his west-facing window, made his thin body appear as if it was cast from bronze, but it also accentuated the wounds from a life-time of being a warrior and a scout. Bullet and stab wounds, cuts and welts, burns and stitching marks criss-crossed his body like a map of all his years.

When we'd been walking our horses from the Silver Spur to the livery, One Leg's limp was so bad that Jia had suggested she try an ancient Chinese procedure on him. It was something her mother had taught her and involved the needles.

'She was *Wu*,' I'd told One Leg.

'*Wu?*' he'd said.

I nodded and gave him my best serious look.

'*Wu*,' he said again, as if he'd understood. The thing was, he'd drunk several whiskies, and that wasn't helping his walk or his judgement much.

'Anything that might help is worth a try,' he said.

I must admit I was keen to see the needles, too. Especially if they were being used on someone else.

So, now he was naked and a young Chinese girl was about to stick those needles in him.

'Are you sure about this?' I asked One Leg, giving him a get-out should he want it.

'Are *you* sure?' he asked Jia.

'Be still. Don't move,' she said.

One Leg's wife, whose name was Grey Fox, was standing over by the window watching. She started grinning, laughing almost, as Jia pressed a needle into One Leg's shoulder. The skin dimpled and then the needle broke the surface and slid into One Leg's flesh. It was the first time since we'd met her that Grey Fox looked remotely happy.

'Does it hurt?' she asked.

'Not yet,' One Leg said, adjusting his position on the hard table. Secretly, and probably needles aside, I think he was enjoying the situation he'd found himself in.

Jia said, 'Don't move.' On the table next to One Leg was a small wallet bound with black leather and lined with soft red velvet. There appeared to be upwards of twenty of the tiny silver needles in the case. Each needle had a thin ivory handle.

Grey Fox pouted.

'You want it to hurt?' I asked her.

'Not really,' she said. 'But he's always talking

about how brave he is. If it hurt it would be his chance to show that bravery.'

Jia slipped another needle in to One Leg's back about six inches below the first. She twisted the needle slightly as it penetrated his skin. Both needles vibrated in the air as he breathed.

'That one?' Grey Fox asked.

'Didn't feel it,' One Leg said. He might have even been telling the truth.

'Can I put one in,' Grey Fox said, stepping away from the window and moving closer to the table where her husband lay. 'I bet I could make him squeal.'

'I'm sure you could,' Jia said, slipping another needle into One Leg's back, this one lower down where his skinny waist looked like he'd been badly burned long ago. 'It's easy to make them hurt. The hard thing is to then take away pain.' Then she said to Grey Fox, 'You're in my light.'

Grey Fox's smile vanished and her face turned hard and expressionless once more.

'How does it work?' I asked. I had a tin cup of whiskey in my hand. One Leg had brought a bottle from the barman at the Silver Spur with some of his winnings. I sipped the whiskey and enjoyed the warm feeling as the drink slid down my throat.

Jia looked up. She was holding a needle in her hand. It picked up a ray of sunlight and sparkled. It reminded me of the way the sunlight reflected off the blades on the roosters' legs. 'It's like moving rocks from a path,' Jia said. 'It clears the way and lets everything flow easy.'

She lifted a corner of the cloth that covered One Leg's behind, and eased the needle into his buttock. I swear he smiled.

'Whiskey does the same thing for me,' I said.

Jia looked at me and said, 'No, it doesn't. You just think it does.'

Then she took another few needles from the velvet case and started working down the other side of One Leg's back.

I finished my whiskey about the same time as Jia slipped the last few needles into One Leg's thigh. Grey Fox, seemingly bored with the fact that her husband wasn't squealing in pain, was over by the stove chopping potatoes, onions, and chicken. Halfway through the procedure One Leg had actually started snoring.

'Looks like a porcupine,' I said quietly. 'Hibernating.'

One Leg Hawk woke up a few minutes later and then Jia took the needles out as slowly and as carefully as she had inserted them.

'How do you feel?' I asked him after he had climbed off the table and dressed. The food Grey Fox was cooking smelled good and Jia had asked her to boil a pan of water in which to clean the needles.

'I don't know,' he said. 'I feel like I've slept all night.'

'It was just five minutes,' Grey Fox said. 'You were snoring.'

'Tomorrow,' Jia said, 'you will notice the difference.'

'Will I be able to dance?' One Leg said.

Over by the stove Grey Fox laughed.

'Maybe,' Jia said.

'It's a long time since I've done a war dance.'

'Do you need to do one?' I said.

'You're going after Schmidt?' One Leg asked me.

'Yes.'

'Then I need to do a war dance.'

Jia and I slept on blankets on the floor of the main room. One Leg and Grey Fox slept in a small second room that had been added to the back of their cabin. For breakfast, Grey Fox made us coffee and tea and biscuits and whilst we ate One Leg told us that, last he heard, Moose Schmidt was in a town called Mustang.

'Actually, it's not a town,' he said. 'It's not even a village. 'It's just a string of buildings along a creek. Not much there at all. But Schmidt has friends and they look out for him.'

He told us where Mustang was and then he looked at the gun that Jia was strapping on, and said, 'Can you use that?'

'I prefer to fight with my hands. But I've practised with the gun. It's a double-action,' she said proudly, glancing at me.

'You prefer hands?' One Leg smiled. Long ago he'd preferred to fight hand to hand, too. It was the warrior way.

'Yes. That's what I'm good at.'

One Leg's smile straightened and he said, 'If you get close enough to Moose Schmidt to fight with your hands, then you're too close.'

I recalled my mother's words all that time ago: *You don't talk and you don't ask questions, and you don't get to wondering on anything. You just shoot him like he did your father. Then you come home.*

One Leg said, 'When you get to the heights north of Green Springs look back. You'll see smoke rising from the yard here.' He looked me straight in the eye. 'I wasn't joking about the war dance.'

# 9

We rode and we talked, letting the horses pick their own way through the tall grass and along the blue-coloured rock trails that crossed this edge of the prairie. When the early summer sun reached its height and the day was too hot for both us and the animals we found shade in an oak forest that lined a narrow river. We rested and watered ourselves and the horses. Jia told me more of her life in China, of the Taiping revolution of which I knew nothing. She wasn't sure what was happening in her home-land now, but a few years before it sounded like vast armies had been marching across the country, bat-tling each other, killing thousands – maybe millions of people. Women, she said, had been burned to death in great numbers, and it was one reason she had learned to fight so well. But no matter how well you could fight there were still some things you couldn't beat. That led her on to tell me of her family's travels across Europe to London and a place called Limehouse. It was an unforgiving place, dark and dreary, wet and cold, and the Londoners were not at all friendly. But it was much safer than China.

Jia's life was full and rich, even though it was filled with hardship and tragedy, and when she asked me about my life I had little to say in comparison. I talked about my father and how things had been with him. I talked of my days and nights in the hills hunting and practising shooting. Jia told me I was too serious. About the practising, I asked, because she'd said she'd done the same with her fighting. No, about life, she said. She told me I should smile and laugh more. I thought about this and realized I had stopped smiling and laughing when Moose Schmidt had killed my father and I realized that I would never be happy unless I killed Schmidt. She said she knew how I felt; but I was handsome when I smiled; and anyway didn't it make me feel better? I allowed that it did.

As the afternoon wore on and cooled a little we again rode towards Mustang, which was still more than a day away. In the distance there were buzzards circling over something.

'How are we going to kill him?' Jia asked, looking at the birds.

I thought of One Leg saying that Schmidt had friends in Mustang. I was starting to feel a knot in my belly. It was small but it grew with every mile that we rode.

'I'd like him to know why we're killing him,' I said. 'But it might not be possible. It will more'n likely have to be quick.'

Maybe that belly-knot was creating a tremor in my voice, for she said, 'I will do it.'

'It's OK.'

'No, it's not an offer. He killed my father and my mother and my cousin. I will do it.'

'He killed my father, too. I need to kill him.'

'As do I.'

'Then we should do it together,' I said. 'We should find out where he lives, maybe watch until he's alone, and then go and do it. Together.'

'And if he's never alone?'

'Let's see when we get there. He will have to be alone sometime.'

She thought about it for a moment and said, 'In the outhouse.'

'What?'

'He will be alone in the outhouse.'

I looked across at her and she wasn't smiling. She was serious. She was still watching the distant buzzards.

'The outhouse?' I said. 'We will kill him in the outhouse?'

She looked at me and held my gaze. 'It's a better plan than you've got.'

The sun was far over in the western quarter. The sky was clear and the distant hills seemed to have flattened in the heat-haze. A shimmering horizon stretched away on either side of us. The prairie here had turned into short-grass scrubland. There were few trees and plants. No animals other than the birds of prey. It felt like we had been, and would be, riding across this vastness for ever. Trying to formulate a plan in such a place was hard. I needed to see something in front of me, the buildings, the people, the way the trails and tracks led in and out of the settlement. I needed to see Moose Schmidt's outhouse.

'The outhouse is one plan,' I said, and forced myself to smile. I wondered if it made me look handsome.

She smiled back.

'It's a good plan.'

We camped in a copse of trees, not far from a creek. The monotonous land had started to undulate a little just before dusk. The trees grew taller. I shot a rabbit with my rifle. We made a fire and cooked the meat and this time we had rice rather than potatoes and Jia used some of her spices and it tasted a whole lot better than my cooking. We fed and watered the horses and we washed in the creek, giving each other privacy, and we both drank tea and we talked some more, laughing as we recalled One Leg grinning secretly as he lay naked on the table the evening before. I took some time cleaning and loading her gun for her. Then we slept beneath the stars. In the middle of the night it grew cold and Jia carried her blanket across to where I was sleeping. She lay down against me and covered us both with her blanket. I listened to her breathing and she wrapped an arm around me. I think she did it in her sleep.

Late the next day we arrived at Mustang.

The town was deceptive in the dusk.

We looked down upon it from a ridge, hidden by pines, but close. At first glance it appeared Mustang was just a handful of buildings straddling a rough track that one would be hard-pushed to get a horse and cart along. There was a burned out lodge at the nearest edge, a few cabins, and then a larger two-storey building with a veranda running round the outside of the first floor. Then came several false-fronted structures and a few more log cabins. But the more we looked, the more we saw. There were other houses and sheds back from the main road, and a couple higher up on the slopes. In the distance, on the hill side, was a cluster of bigger buildings. Maybe a mine, or a mill, I thought. On closer inspection I saw the roof appeared to have collapsed. It was in a state of disrepair. In fact, Mustang as a whole looked to be in a state of disrepair.

It was surely too warm for the residents to have many fires lit, but smoke curled upwards from the chimney in one of the huts midway between us and the town centre, if the place could be described as such. More smoke came from the chimney of one of the false-fronted buildings. As the night darkened, lights became apparent through the windows of that false-fronted building, and when the breeze blew towards us I could hear voices and laughter and, I fancied, a piano. The saloon, I guessed. A dog meandered along the street, sniffing at this and that, and a woman and a man came out of the saloon, hand in hand, and walked a few yards down to the two-storey building. I picked out horses tied to a rail a few buildings further into town. There were wagons parked along the side of the street.

There were several piles of rough lumber on a track that ran off the main road, and if I followed that track upwards it disappeared into the treeline on the far side of the valley. More lights appeared. I saw a few more people walking towards the saloon. I saw a man come out the back of the bar and go into the outhouse in the yard. I saw two Indians come out of the building just beyond the saloon and climb onto the two horses. They said something to each other, one of them leaned over and appeared to spit on the ground, and then they rode out of town, in the direction away from Jia and I.

It looked like a town that was struggling to survive but was just holding on.

'Do you know what Moose Schmidt looks like?' Jia whispered.

'I have a Wanted poster with a drawing of him. It's a few years old but I know his face. You told me he has a limp. I know from One Leg that he is a big man, tall and heavy and muscular.'

'My mother described him to me in her letters,' Jia said. 'Yes, he is big and has a limp. He walks with a stick, she said, and leans his weight to the right. He moves slowly. He had a beard – maybe still does – and dark hair with grey in it that was bushy and curly. Blue eyes. *Bright* blue eyes.'

'Would you like to see the poster?' I asked.

'Yes.'

I went back into the trees where we had left the horses. The poster was folded up carefully in the bottom of a saddlebag. I took the picture back to Jia and in the light of the rising moon we looked down upon the face of the man we had come to kill.

'My mother wrote that he wears a gun on his left hip, despite being right-handed.'

'His right hand is holding his stick,' I said.

'Yes,' she said. Then: 'Do you think he's down there?'

I looked again at the darkening town. The air was cooler now and the piano music was much clearer.

'One Leg said this is where he is.'

She looked at me and in the moonlight her skin was as smooth and as perfect as a gold satin dress that my father had once bought my mother. Her eyes were as deep and dark as a well.

'And we're going to kill him together?'

'Yes,' I said, feeling that knot getting ever bigger in my stomach.

\*

Our plan was to watch, and if it took a whole day, so be it. If it took two days, so be it. We had both waited years already. If Moose Schmidt was here we would see him, and watch him, and when we knew where he lived we would do what we needed to do.

At one point Jia took delight in pointing out to me that almost every cabin in Mustang had an out-house. We laughed quietly in the dark trees and looked at each other's silhouettes and she reached out and touched my arm and I tried to understand if there was something more than revenge happening here.

But before I could think on it any further, we saw Moose Schmidt limping through Mustang towards us.

It had to be Moose. A big man with a stick, leaning heavily to the right. He had the beard and he was here in Mustang.

What were the odds that it was someone else?

He shuffled along Main Street in our direction, the moonlight illuminating him, paused outside a cabin that, apart from the one that was burned out, was the closest one to us, and he looked up at the clear night sky. He turned around very slowly as if examining the stars. At one point he was looking directly at us, but I knew we were invisible in the trees. Then he turned and went into the cabin.

My heart was racing. My hands felt cold and damp. I breathed through my mouth, taking the air deep into my chest, trying to calm myself.

It was Moose Schmidt for sure.

We were so close to the man that had killed our kin.

'He looks old,' Jia whispered.

'And he's alone,' I said. 'Unless someone else had been in that cabin ever since we got here.'

'There's been no smoke.'

'It's not too cold,' I said.

'People still cook in the evening,' Jia said. 'And anyway it does get cold at night.'

'So, he could be alone.'

'And he looks old,' she said again. I thought of the roosters fighting and of Reuben giving out odds. Did the fact that Moose looked old make our own odds better?

'Let's sit tight,' I said. 'Let the town go to sleep.'

'Then?'

'Then we'll go down there and do it.'

We waited two, maybe three, hours. We'd been prepared to wait for days so a few hours was easy. The moon moved gently along the line of the Mustang valley. The night did grow cold, but we were sweating with anticipation of what lay ahead.

I'd like to say I considered – and questioned – how easy it had been to find him. But it didn't cross my mind.

When there had been no movement – except for animals – in Mustang for what seemed like an hour, I whispered to Jia, 'Let's do it.'

We slipped out of the cover of the trees and very slowly, very carefully, and very silently we eased our-selves down the slope and into Mustang.

We paused, hidden behind the burnt-out skele-ton of the cabin next door to the one that we had seen Moose go into. We waited some more. There was no movement. Mustang was sleeping soundly.

So we crept forwards to Moose Schmidt's cabin.

Moose Schmidt was snoring.

I glanced at Jia. She was in the dark shadows outside Schmidt's cabin. I couldn't see her expres-sion, just the gleam of moonlight on her cheek bones. I pressed lightly on Schmidt's door. It was latched. I reached out and lifted the latch. It squeaked, but it was the quietest of squeaks. Schmidt carried on snoring.

I pushed against the door again. It was a heavy door. I noticed that there were old brackets midway up that would have once held a hefty piece of timber to bar the door. It looked as if the door had been taken from somewhere else and reused on this house. Maybe from the mill upon the hill that had looked abandoned?

I pressed harder and the heavy door eased opened an inch.

There was the slightest rub of wood on wood, but

nothing loud.

Another inch.

My right hand rested on my gun. Jia already had hers drawn.

I pushed the door further open, it swung easily now on oiled hinges and I had to hold back its weight so it didn't swing all the way through its arc and crash into the inside wall. The room smelled musty as if it hadn't been aired in a long time. I felt the interior warmth against my face.

I forced myself to breathe slowly, but my heart was beating so wildly I felt sure it would wake Schmidt.

I could see inside the house now. It was dark, but moonlight shone through a window and illuminated a large kitchen-come-living room. Where the thick window frames blocked the light, a crucifix-shaped shadow was cast across the room. There was an unlit stove, a table, chairs, a kitchen bench. There were two dishes on the table, a bottle of whiskey, half empty. Nothing more. It was sparsely furnished and I figured Schmidt must live alone. There was a single door set in the far wall.

I took my first step into the house.

The snoring stopped.

I froze.

I looked back at Jia. The moonlight on her face made it look like she had cat's eyes.

Moose Schmidt started snoring again.

I waited a minute, maybe more, then I took

another step inside. I motioned for Jia to stay outside, but she shook her head. She wanted to kill Moose as badly as I. We'd talked about waiting until he went to the outhouse. It was right there around the back of his house, a small shed surrounded by vast piles of brushwood, and cut logs, as if Schmidt had spent most of the summer so far preparing for winter. But, we'd agreed, he probably had a pot under his bed, and would be unlikely to use the outhouse until morning, and we wanted to get this done now. It's not an easy thing to work yourself up to a point where you can shoot a man dead, but it's a lot easier in the darkness. The town was sleeping, too. That said, it wasn't something I was sure I could do, and I wasn't sure Jia could either. I'd been thinking of my father, and of all those other men Moose had killed, trying to build up a head of killing steam. I thought of Moose shooting Jia's mother in the back, of how he'd gone about killing her father and cousin, almost playing with them the way a cat played with a mouse once he had it cornered. It ought to be easy to kill a man like that. We'd be doing everyone else a favour. How many lives would we ultimately save by killing him? But still my bones felt chilled, my hands wet, and my throat dry. Maybe if he saw us? Maybe if he drew on me? Maybe if I was to look him in the eye it would be easier?

I took another step.

That walk across his kitchen was the longest,

slowest, walk that I've ever made. For a while clouds obscured the moonlight and Jia and I were plunged into a darkness that made my breathing and heartbeat feel even louder.

Eventually, I reached the inside door, and as I extended my hand to open it Moose stopped snoring again. I hesitated, and I imagined I felt something cold caress me. The chill crept over my skin like the touch of a ghost. I looked at Jia and could see that she'd felt it too.

I heard something scraping.

Wood against wood?

Then moonlight filled the room again and with it the realization that we were deep inside the killer's house. We'd come this far. We had to finish it.

I waited for the snoring to start again.

It didn't.

I had no choice. I pushed open the inside door.

Moose Schmidt was asleep on a mattress with an Indian blanket over him. His back was to me. There was indeed a pot by the window, so the outhouse plan would have meant waiting until morning and daylight. A candle burned on the floor next to Schmidt's head. I recall thinking briefly how dangerous that was – a candle burning down on the dry timber floor as he slept. Maybe he'd been too drunk to remember to blow it out. Although the candle was in a silver candleholder placed upon a saucer, so I guess it wasn't too much of a risk. A man like Schmidt didn't grow old by taking risks.

Jia stood next to me.

I slid my gun out of my holster, and I pulled the hammer back, the sound of the ratchet loud in the stillness of that room.

Schmidt didn't wake.

I knew I couldn't do this whilst he was asleep, no matter how much of a risk it was to wake him.

Jia never felt the same.

She shot him. Once, twice, three times. The gunshots deafening in the small room. Flames blazed from the barrel of her revolver. The smell of cordite and gunpowder filled the room in an instant. Smoke billowed around us both and dust rose from the blanket that had been covering Schmidt. Part of the blanket began to smoulder where the red hot lead had passed through it. Another part of the blanket was lifted and moved by the force of the bullets.

Underneath was a feed sack stuffed with something that made it resemble the shape of a man.

There was no sign of Moose Schmidt.

# 10

I ran to the window and gave it a tug. It wouldn't open and I realized now that something was blocking the moonlight from the outside. I looked at Jia. She stood still, totally confused. She had just killed a man – or so she thought – and yet a moment later he wasn't even there. All that emotion and reaction became incomprehension. She went over to the try the window too.

I rushed into the kitchen and I heard Schmidt laughing at the same time as I heard him dropping a length of timber into the brackets on the outside of the front door.

'You thought you were lucky, no?' he said, chuckling. 'The fish thinks it's lucky when it finds the juicy worm.' He laughed again, and I heard something being pushed up against the bottom of the door on the outside. 'Then it finds the hook, too.'

Jia came back into the kitchen. She was shaking her head. Maybe in disbelief, maybe to clear the confusion. The smell of gun smoke came with her from the bedroom. 'The window won't open. It's nailed or blocked on the outside. And there's a hole in the inside wall.'

'A hole?'

She pointed to the wall. I saw a small black oval. It looked like a knot in the wood.

'He must have been watching us as we crept across the kitchen.'

Her eyes were wide and she was beginning to breathe rapidly. I'd already examined the kitchen window, but she checked it again. The frame that cast the crucifix shadow wasn't a window frame but was two wide lengths of wood that had been nailed on the outside. They were broad enough to prevent us using that window as a means of escape.

'The door?' she said.

I shook my head.

'Then we're trapped.' I knew Moose Schmidt heard because he started laughing again.

Jia heard him. She looked young and frightened.

It took me a moment to realize what Schmidt was doing. His laughter came and went, and I heard him talking to someone else. I heard the rustle of something against the outside wall of the house. There was a pause, then I heard more of whatever it was being laid up against the house.

I was sweating and I was shaking, but a chill froze the marrow in my bones.

I pictured the shack next door – the burned

down shack. I saw those piles of brushwood and cut logs and dry branches up against the outhouse. Schmidt hadn't been saving them for summer. He had been saving them for us.

'What is it?' Jia said, seeing something terrible in my eyes.

I shook my head.

'*What is it?*' she demanded.

Then we heard the crackle of flames.

It wouldn't have happened to my father. It wouldn't have happened to One Leg Hawk. But what did we know, Jia and I? We were just kids. My father and One Leg would never have walked into that trap the way we did. Certainly, if there had been two of them, they wouldn't have *both* gone into the house. They wouldn't have both taken the bait. One of them would have been outside right now and things would have been OK.

Or, if not OK, a whole lot better.

The breeze we had felt hadn't been a ghost. It had been Moose slipping out of the window. It was barred now, as we had found out. He'd had it all ready – watch us, pretend to snore, and then at just the right moment a quick escape. After that, run around to the door and drop the barrier in place. The wooden slots I'd seen in the front door weren't there because it was an old door that had been reused; they had been fixed there to allow a beam to be dropped quickly in place, locking us in. It had all been in front of me and I had missed it. We had both missed it. The lack of furniture and possessions that I had put down to Moose being a man living alone had actually been because he didn't live here. The whole place was a trap, nothing else.

'The fellow next door – you saw the burned out shack? – he screamed for twenty minutes,' Moose said from somewhere just outside the kitchen window.

I fired a bullet through the wall towards his voice and I heard him laughing.

'He was a bounty hunter,' Moose said. 'He was a sorry sonofabitch.'

I fired another bullet and he laughed again.

Smoke was finding its way in through the tiny gaps where logs and planks of wood met. The moonlight shining into the room was growing hazy now, and outside the flames reached up to the window.

Sweat rolled down my face, my back, and my sides.

Jia came in again from the bedroom where she had desperately been looking for something – a loose board, a gap in the roof, *anything*. She shook her head. 'There's no way out.'

'I knew you were coming,' Moose said, and as he spoke on one side of the house I could hear someone else piling brushwood up against the other. 'Knew as soon as you left St Mary's. I got eyes

98

and ears all over.'

Jia was blinking rapidly now. I don't know if it was the smoke or panic or tears.

'What are we going to?' she said.

'I heard you were at the bird fight,' Moose said. 'With that crippled old Indian. I could have killed him many times, but sometimes leaving them alive is just as much fun.'

It was getting too hot. Over by the window where I think Moose had first set the fire I could see the wood glowing red. The flames would catch on the inside, soon.

Jia tried the door again.

It was as solid as it had been when we had both pushed against it minutes earlier.

Jia was panting for breath. My hair was soaking with sweat.

Now the wood over by the window did burst alight.

'Cal,' Jia said, shaking her head, her eyes wide.

'I figured,' Moose said, his voice a little further along the wall now, 'I might go and see your mother next. Well, fact is. I've already been. Saw you too, Cal. Though neither of you knew I was there. Folks say your ma is the prettiest woman in the territory, and I tend to agree with them. Well, of her age, anyway. And that's my kind of age. Yes, I think I might go and see her. You think on that, Callum Johnson. You think on that as you burn.'

*

The room filled with smoke. It was hot enough that we had to keep lifting our feet, dancing like bear cubs on hot tin plates. It was almost impossible to breathe. The smoke scorched our lungs as we inhaled. Tears streamed down Jia's face. She was holding onto me, her fingers digging in like claws. Her eyes darted around the room wildly. There was nothing we could do. We'd kicked every wall, wrenched both windows with all our strength, and we'd smashed the door with our shoulders. All to no avail. Now the fire was sucking the energy from us and it was all we could do to stand in the centre of the room, turning, looking this way and that, around and around, in the desperate hope that a wall would collapse before we were burned alive.

Jia started mumbling something in Chinese. It may have been a prayer. She pressed herself harder against me and looked up at me but I don't think she was seeing me any longer, or at least she wasn't focusing on me. She was looking beyond me, at an eternity that was forming somewhere deep inside the fire and the smoke.

I was weeping, too, tears streaming down my face from the hot smoke that was burning my eyes. I coughed and choked. My tears evaporated in the heat. I pulled a neckerchief over my face and I indicated to Jia that she should do the same. It was too hot to talk. It was noisy, as well; flames were roaring and crackling and heavy timbers shrieked as their weight shifted in the furnace. I found myself thinking of my mother, and of my father, trying to conjure up images of them. I pictured the boarding house back in St Mary's Gap. I remembered the time my father and I met Jia's mother in Natchez. I imagined fishing and swimming in cool refreshing water. I thought of those fighting birds back in Green Springs. I thought of the rooster named General dying in its handler's arms, of the way that bird's helpless eyes had looked as it faced death. I thought of how, just a few minutes ago, Jia and I had been up on the hill looking down on the sleeping town of Mustang and I cursed the fact that if only we hadn't both come down here and both crept inside this house, we would still be all right.

*If only.*

Now flames started dripping from the ceiling. I brushed several burning embers from Jia's hair. Still holding each other, we edged away from the place where the ceiling was raining fire on us, but the terrible reality was that there was nowhere else to go.

I noticed that the hem of Jia's coat was burning. I reached down and batted at the smouldering material and immediately I felt an intense pain on the back of my neck.

Jia brushed a burning fragment off my skin. I flicked smoking ash from her boots. But more ash and fire and embers were falling all the time. It was like trying to avoid snowflakes in a blizzard.

Jia gasped loudly and involuntarily – in fear or in

pain, I wasn't sure. But it didn't matter. I knew in a few minutes, probably less, we would both be screaming.

Outside, I could still hear Moose Schmidt laughing, although it might have been echoes inside my head. Surely he would have had to move away from the inferno.

But no, there he was again. Real laughter. Real enjoyment.

I drew my gun as the fire closed in on us. If I did nothing else I would do my best to shoot Schmidt through the burning walls. Maybe, now that he thought our end was near, he might have stopped moving.

Keep laughing, I thought, trying to take a bead on his voice.

Just keep laughing.

The gunshot came before I pulled the trigger.

My mind was running so slowly that I didn't really comprehend what I'd heard. Panic and fear, pain and hopelessness, had seized me. It felt like everything – my life force, my bodily functions, my ability to think – had been squeezed to the point of no return. I was shutting down.

I willed myself to shoot, determined that my final act in this life would be to try and avenge mine and Jia's imminent death.

But my muscles wouldn't respond.

Somewhere inside came the realization that I was

drowning, not burning. Or rather it was both. I couldn't breathe, and whether the situation was caused by fire or water was wholly irrelevant.

I felt Jia slump against my body. I tried to hold her upright.

I heard the gunshot again. And another.

Now I realized what I was hearing and the fact puzzled me.

How could there be gunshots when I hadn't pulled the trigger?

Suddenly the door of the house was flung open, and with it came a rush of cold fresh air and the flames all around us were blown backwards for a moment and I saw a shape, a man, in the doorway. He was crouched down holding and firing a rifle.

'Get out!' he cried.

He worked the action on his rifle and fired again. I heard other gunfire, too.

'Get out!'

The man glanced at me and I saw from the shape of his head and his hat that it was One Leg Hawk. More questions filled my mind.

'Callum!' he cried. 'Get out!'

Somehow I found the strength to move, to drag Jia towards the door, towards that cool air. Behind me the fire raining down from the roof of the cabin turned into a storm – all those embers and burning fragments loosened by that blast of incoming air.

Then I was at the door and I was breathing again, gasping for oxygen like a fish that had been out of water for too long. I saw that One Leg had a pistol out now. Smoke was billowing all around him, hiding him.

'I brought the horses down,' he said. 'Go!'

I felt a bullet whistle through the air between us. I could hear Jia coughing and choking, but at least she was breathing. I still had my revolver in my hand and I shot in the same general direction as One Leg was shooting, through the smoke, through the flames, into the blackness beyond. I fanned the hammer just like Samuel Johnson had taught me so long ago.

'Go!' One Leg yelled again. He was crouching now, still firing, but edging backwards into the billowing clouds of wood smoke coming from the door.

I fired again. The hammer came down on an empty chamber.

Then I felt something cut through my leg, a bright and intense pain amongst all the darker agonies that were raging from every muscle.

I was still able to move so I ignored the new pain and pulled Jia backwards. A few yards from the house the smoke cleared and there were our horses, three of them, standing there in the cool night air, trembling with fear at the fire and the noise and the gunshots, but standing there, nonetheless. Jia bent over, retching, and a bullet sliced through the air where her head would have been had she been upright.

I heard One Leg curse as his revolver hammer came down on an empty chamber too. Then I heard him grunt in pain.

A second later he was alongside me, heaving Jia onto her horse as if she was a sack of feed, slapping the horse's rump and sending it skittering up the hill into the night, Jia aware enough to hold onto something – anything. Then One Leg was helping me up on my horse, too.

I heard the explosion and whistle of another gunshot.

I heard One Leg hiss with pain, but then he was on his horse too and the pair of us were racing after Jia, the smoke from the burning house like a wall behind us, creating an impenetrable curtain across the track, the very thing that was going to kill us now shielding us.

# 11

I have no idea how long we rode for before the horses slowed, and eventually came to a standstill. It may have been fifteen minutes; it may have been an hour. I was in a daze. My mind was racing even more widely and randomly than it had done whilst in the burning house. There were moments when I thought I was back in that inferno. Other times I found myself gasping for air as if I was still suffocating. I remember trying to talk to Jia and One Leg, shouting to them, my throat hoarse, my voice weak and lacking volume. I don't recall them answering. So we raced on and I think we may have all ridden all night had the horses not decided otherwise.

We stopped deep in a gully. There were trees silhouetted on the skyline, stars visible behind them. I could smell smoke and it took me a terrible minute before I realized that nothing was burning, that my clothes were impregnated with the stench of fire.

The horses were foaming at the mouths and they were slick with sweat. Their chests heaved and I could feel my horse trembling with the effort it had put in.

I looked over my shoulder, convinced that they – Moose Schmidt and his friends – would be there, just a few horse lengths behind us, guns drawn.

Nobody was there. We were alone.

That didn't mean they weren't coming, but we had ridden fast and hard. Whether they were out there or not, we had to rest. The horses couldn't go on.

'Did we kill him?' Jia asked.

It was the first thing she had said since almost falling unconscious in the flames. At some point during the ride, early on, I assumed, she had pulled herself upright on her horse.

I shook my head. 'I don't know.'

I looked over at One Leg. He'd lost his hat, the blue felt hat I'd first seen him wearing at the cock fight and had recognized when he had flung open the door of Schmidt's house. His head was lowered as if it was too heavy for his neck muscles. His dark hair hung down over his cheeks.

'One Leg?' I said.

Slowly he turned towards me. His face looked yellow in the moonlight.

'I think I might have shot him,' he said. His mouth stayed open after he'd spoken as if closing it would take too much effort.

'How. . . ?' Jia said. I don't think she was asking how he'd shot Moose, but how had he found us.

One Leg closed his eyes. I saw his chest was heaving.

'One Leg?' I said.

'Help me off the horse,' he said. 'I need to lie down.'

'Are you OK?'

'I think I shot him,' he said, and before I could dismount and get to him, he slid sideways off his horse and slammed into the ground.

One Leg was still breathing when I got to him. I raised his head gently, just enough to get my hand under the back of his skull, to lift it from the hard ground, to hold him.

'One Leg,' I said. 'It's OK. Lie still.' Not that he was able to move.

His eyes were closed. The lids flickered briefly but behind them were just the whites of his eyes. He convulsed, but it was the slightest of convulsions as if his body didn't even have the strength for that.

I held him a moment longer then lowered his head, and not knowing what else to do I looked over my shoulder. Jia was off her horse and coming towards us.

'Water,' I said.

She shook her head. 'Water might not be the best thing.'

I saw how wet One Leg's coat was. My hands came away slick and dark and when I opened his jacket there was so much blood that his shirt was pasted to him as if he'd been caught in a thunderstorm.

He shuddered again. The tiniest of shudders.

The bullet had hit him square in the chest. It was as close to being a heart shot as I could imagine.

'It's going to be OK,' I said. But I looked up at Jia and I shook my head.

When I looked back at One Leg I realized he was too still, the slight moving of his breathing had stopped. There was no flicker behind his eyelids, no shudders, no convulsions.

'No,' I said. 'No.'

He had saved our lives. He couldn't leave us. Not now. Not after everything.

I felt Jia's hand on my shoulder. She knew.

'One Leg,' I said, the words obscured by something caught in my throat. 'One Leg.'

I leant my face close to his. I prayed that I would feel breath on my cheek. I turned my head, praying to hear that breath.

But there was no breath felt or heard.

One Leg was gone.

Later, the more I thought on it, the more I realized it had been an instant-killing shot. One Leg Hawk should have died there and then outside that burning house. The bullet wound was huge and devastating. No one could take a shot like that and even stand up. Yet he had pushed Jia onto her horse, had helped me up, and then had ridden with us at full pace for however long it had been.

It was impossible.

But he had done it.

And when we were safe, only then had he allowed himself to die.

Jia and I held each other and we let tears come. For a while it felt like the tears wouldn't stop. But the very fact of One Leg's death, the smell of smoke on our clothes, and the burns and pains we had ourselves suffered reminded us that Mustang, and the people there, were only a few miles away.

We couldn't stay here, not in the open, not in a gully like this.

So, somehow, we managed to wrap One Leg in his blanket and tie him onto his horse. I reloaded our guns and we remounted and we rode slowly and in silence, out of the gully, and toward some dark tree-lined hills in the distance.

Again, time seemed to have no substance, and when eventually we reached the trees and stopped deep inside the cover, I had no concept of how much of the night remained.

We laid One Leg's body on the ground and we drank water from our skins and I filled my singed hat with water and let the horses drink. I tethered them loosely where the grass was good and then I came back to where Jia was sitting on a blanket.

'You're limping,' she said. Her voice sounded quiet and tired and flat in the darkness.

'I'm OK.' I had forgotten about the bullet that had cut through my leg back at the house.

'Let me see.'

'I'm OK.'

But now that she'd mentioned it, I did feel the pain in my leg. A pain sharper than everything else I felt in the rest of my exhausted body.

I sat down beside Jia. She reached out for me.

'Your trousers are soaked in blood.'

'I can't believe he's dead,' I said.

There was a moment's silence and then Jia said, 'He said he thought he'd shot Schmidt.'

'Yes.'

'We need to know.'

'We need to take One Leg home. We will soon hear if Schmidt is dead.'

'And if he's not, then we will kill him.' It wasn't a question.

I nodded in the darkness. One Leg Hawk was another on a growing list of people we needed to avenge.

'Your boot is full of blood,' Jia said. 'We need to take it off.'

'I'm fine.'

But she was already pulling at my boot and although my foot itself wasn't hurt, the leg above the boot screamed when she did that.

Once the boot was off she put it to one side and

then removed the other.

'You need to take your trousers off. Either that or I need to cut them. And aside from all that blood and a couple of bullet holes they look pretty good to me.'

I tried to come up with something funny in response but my mind was blank. So I undid my gun belt and I placed the gun in easy reach, and then I undid my trouser belt and the buttons and I started to work the trousers down. Where my blood had clotted it had glued the frayed material into my wounded flesh and now, as I tore the trousers free, it felt like a dozen white-hot knife blades had all been inserted into my right calf. I inhaled sharply and held the air inside in my lungs. I squeezed my eyes closed and I heard Jia whisper, 'It's OK, Cal.' Then she was pulling my trousers down over the wound and the worst of it was past. I felt cold air on my legs and I breathed again. I shivered and I lay back and rested my head on the ground and looked up at the trees and, between the branches I saw a few stars, and I thought of One Leg Hawk, and of my father.

Jia poured cold water over the wound and it stung worse than the bullet had stung. I raised my head to look at her and saw her taking her jacket off. She was wearing a man's shirt. In the darkness I couldn't tell what colour, although I must have known because we'd been riding together for two days. She undid the shirt buttons and then she

112

slipped it off just as the moonlight found its way between trees. She wore a thin white sleeveless top under the shirt, and in the moonlight I could see the lines of her body, her shoulders, her breasts, her stomach. The skin on her arms shone and looked so smooth I wanted to reach out and run my fingers down her. She tore first one sleeve off her shirt and then the other. She soaked one of the lengths of cloth in water and she used it to wash and wipe the blood away from my leg.

'I'd like to use hot water,' she said. 'But no fire tonight.'

'No fire,' I said. My heart had started beating a little harder, pushing hot blood throughout my body. She was crouched down with her back to me as she worked on my leg and her white undershirt was riding high. I reached out and touched the small of her back. She shuddered a little. I thought I heard the breath catch in her throat. But it may have been imagination.

'I think the bullet went straight through,' she said. Her voice was soft and a little lower than normal.

I could feel her fingers on my leg, resting there.

I spread my fingers on her back and I could feel her warmth, her softness.

She started to twist around to look at me, but then she turned back and I felt her quickly wrapping the other torn sleeve around my leg, tying it crudely.

113

Then she rested her hand on my leg above the wound, and I could feel her thumb moving slowly, making tiny circles on my skin.

I reached out with my other hand and I held her waist. I could feel her body's movement beneath my hands. She, like me, was breathing faster than we had been just a minute before.

Now she did turn and she looked down upon me and although her face was in darkness I could see the shape of her eyes and her lips and her nose, I could see how her hair was haloed against the moon, and then she leaned forward and she kissed me. Her lips tasted of salt and smoke, of blood and tears. I returned her kiss and then suddenly everything from that night, the anticipation of killing a man, the shooting of what we thought was that man in his bed, the fire, the terror, the relief as One Leg had rescued us, the smoke and the crazy race to safety, and most of all watching One Leg pass away before our eyes, all swept over us and once again time disintegrated and now instinct and a deep human need took over.

We made love and it didn't seem wrong that One Leg's body was lying just yards away. The sudden and unexpected passion helped drive everything else from our minds and bodies. We held each other and we kissed and we moved together as if we were one and it was proof that we were alive and that we had each other, that we each had someone, that for a few minutes amongst all the darkness, we were OK.

And afterwards we held each other and waited for the night to pass.

# 12

A day and a half's riding brought us back to Green Springs. As we approached One Leg's cabin, Grey Fox came outside as if she had been expecting us. From a distance I saw her body language change as she realized there were three horses and only two riders. I saw her reach out for support, not looking, not realizing that there was nothing to hold onto. She fell, crumpling to the ground. I saw her punch the earth several times, and even though we were still a distance away I heard her wailing.

Grey Fox said, 'It was the war dance. As soon as he'd performed it and looked at the smoke, he knew something was wrong. He told me he had to follow you. I said "How? You can't even get on a horse any more." But he could. The needles had made him feel young again.' She looked at us and she smiled. 'You two were fast asleep but we had a good night, that night. After the needles.'

I looked at Jia, and there was such knowledge in our eyes too.

I glanced at the third horse. One Leg's body was still tied across the saddle. 'I'm so sorry,' I said.

Grey Fox looked at her husband's body, too. 'Don't be.' She turned back to me. 'He hated not being a warrior any more. This is the way he would have wanted to go. I expected it.'

'What will you do?' Jia asked.

'I will take him home,' she said. 'To his people.'

'And you?'

'They're my people, too. Even though they weren't happy with him marrying me. They said no good would come of it.'

'He saved our lives,' I said.

'I'm not sure that some of his people will see that as good. I'm sorry to say it.'

'It's OK,' Jia said.

Grey Fox looked over at the horses again. She walked towards them, to her husband's body. Jia and I followed, but we allowed Grey Fox space. She reached out and touched One Leg.

She turned. 'You know he had to fight to win me?'

I shook my head.

'I'm young, yes?'

'Yes.'

'And he was old and they – none of them – were happy. There was a young one. His name was *Wohali* – White Eagle. He was handsome and he was strong

117

and there was a lot to be happy about with a man – a boy – like that.'

She turned again to her husband's body and touched his leg gently.

'This one was old, then,' she said, looking at us again but leaving her hand on One Leg. 'And I knew there was no future. But sometimes . . . well, sometimes it feels like destiny was calling us. He had no money and he was most probably too old for children. But there was something in his eyes and there was something in the way he was with the old and the young, with everyone really. He had been a warrior and there weren't so many of those anymore.'

Tears formed in her eyes.

'And he fought *Wohali*?' Jia asked.

Grey Fox looked at her. 'Yes. I don't think it really was a fight to the death, but that's what they said beforehand. I felt sure I would end up with *Wohali*, and that wouldn't have been bad. In many ways it would have been good. But inside. Here. . . .' She thumped a fist against her breast. 'I knew that I felt more for *Tawodi*. Before the fight started I was already sad for my loss.'

She looked back at One Leg again. 'It's how I feel again now.'

The tears spilled from her eyes.

'*Wohali* – all of them – should have known that *Tawodi* had learned and forgotten more about fighting than the youngsters would ever know. They don't fight any more, do they? They – we – have had the fight beaten from us. But not *Tawodi*.' Grey Fox smiled at the memory. 'He fought hard and fair. His legs might have been slow but his hands were fast and he could read *Wohali*'s mind, or so it seemed. They had knives and though *Wohali* cut *Tawodi* a few times, every time he did so, *Tawodi* cut him twice, maybe three times. And deeper, too.'

I thought of One Leg watching the bird fight just a few days before. It had seemed terribly cruel and pointless to me, but now I understood why One Leg might like it so much.

'Eventually *Wohali* tripped. I think he was tiring, and Tawodi never tired.'

Now Grey Fox looked at Jia and smiled the same smile as she'd done when mentioning the results of the needles a few minutes earlier.

Jia smiled back. 'A man that doesn't tire is a good man.'

Grey Fox held Jia's gaze for a moment. Then she wiped her cheeks with the back of her hand and said, '*Tawodi* could have killed him, but he didn't. He stepped back and he held out his hand and he pulled *Wohali* to his feet. I suspect *Wohali* wished he had been killed. It was a shameful defeat. But then maybe not. *Tawodi* was . . . special.'

'He certainly was,' I said. 'I will never forget him.'

'No,' Grey Fox said. 'Please don't. As long as someone remembers him, as long as someone speaks his name, then he is still alive somewhere.'

We were exhausted, as were the horses. After leaving Grey Fox – gracefully turning down her offer of a place to sleep for the night – we made it only as far as the Silver Spur. We needed food and clothes and to clean and dress my wound properly. We both wanted to wash the smoke from our bodies. But there was an echo of something Moose Schmidt had said still bouncing around inside my head.

'He said he was going to St Mary's Gap,' I said to Jia. 'To see my mother.'

I was drinking whiskey. Jia said she'd try a whiskey, too. It made her cough. But after we'd both finished the first one she'd been happy to have another. I think it surprised her how good it made her feel.

'It was just talk.'

'We don't know that.'

'He thought we were going to die. He was enjoying the moment. He wanted to make it even worse for us than it was. That's what he does. He enjoys it the worse it is.'

'I don't know.'

'And anyway. . . .'

'What?'

'He might be dead. One Leg said. . . .' She let the words tail off. We had both heard One Leg's last words. But had they simply been words of reassurance, rather than fact?

It had been impossible to see anything once we had burst from the house. The thick smoke had been billowing around the doorway and the flames had been like a wall. But One Leg had been there calmly steadying himself and shooting at something.

'Yes,' I said. 'He might be dead. But he might not be.'

'We need a night,' Jia said. 'The horses need a night.'

I drank my whiskey.

'Anyway, St Mary's Gap is not like here,' she said. 'It's not like Mustang. It's . . . civilised. Your mother isn't alone.'

'Another whiskey?' I asked.

'Are we staying?'

'One night,' I said.

'Then I'll have another whiskey,' Jia said.

We shared a room, and we shared a bed, but we didn't make love. It was partly exhaustion and partly drunkenness. But it was also that One Leg was dead, and although that fact had helped ignite our passion the previous night, when our bodies and our minds had needed a release from the emotions of events, tonight the fact made us melancholy and respectful.

So we slept, and in the morning we ate breakfast, and we took our leave of Green Springs, and we headed home.

*

As we rode I told Jia the details of my father's death. She knew some of it, but I filled in the gaps. I told her of how Schmidt had tricked my father and then used his own son as a shield from behind which to shoot. I told her of how I'd seen One Leg at death's door all those years ago, and of how it had seemed to me at the time he'd been fighting so hard to stay alive.

'Sometimes I wonder if it isn't all ordained,' I said. 'Destiny. Like Grey Fox and One Leg.'

'I think so, too.' Jia looked around as we rode, at the distant horizon, the vastness of the landscape, the stunted and dead trees, the dryness of everything. Eventually her eyes landed on me. She smiled and said, '*Yuánfèn.*'

Her smile looked sad to me. I could understand that. Inside I was sad, too, and I'm sure I looked that way on the outside. I could still picture the tears on Grey Fox's cheeks.

'*Yuánfèn?*' I said.

'Fate,' she said. 'It was *yuánfèn* that we found each other.'

But I knew that it wasn't quite like that. We hadn't casually chanced upon each other.

'*You* found *me*,' I said, and she nodded as if the real meaning of *yuánfèn* was indeed something else.

Much later we came upon the old surveyors' huts again. We could have pushed on to St Mary's Gap but we were tired, and the darkness pressed heavily upon us. It was cold, too, and the horses were exhausted even though we had ridden slowly. My leg was hurting and we were both hungry.

The huts looked inviting enough that we stayed. We made a fire and we cooked the food we had bought in Green Springs and we boiled water and drank tea. Jia cleaned my bullet wound again, and though it was still painful, there was no sign of any infection. The bullet had gone through flesh and muscle, tearing me up a little, but not hitting and smashing any bones.

We lay our blankets on the floor of one of the huts, and the moon, just beyond full, cast a silver light across those blankets. Outside, we had talked a lot, but now we were quiet. My arm was around Jia and her head was resting on my chest. I could hear the slowness of her breathing. My heartbeat seemed to adjust itself to match with her rhythms. I kissed her hair and she murmured something. Her hand was resting on my stomach and she slipped it beneath my undershirt and laid it on my skin. She moved her fingers gently and I felt our matched rhythms started to change. She turned her head upwards and in that silver moonlight she was beautiful and young, flawless and yet somehow so heart-breakingly sad. We kissed and her lips were soft and moist and her hand pressed harder against me.

It was the most natural thing in the world to make love. It was different to the first time. Then it had been an affirmation that we were still alive. It had been a release from the fear and the closeness of death, both our own and One Leg's. This time it was much more about each other, about knowing each other, discovering each other. We weren't shy and we weren't rushed and it was the most physically wonderful thing that had happened to me in my life. But underneath it all, even as it felt as good as I could imagine anything in this world could ever feel – and I knew Jia was experiencing that wonder, too – there was something else.

It felt like the end of something, not the beginning.

We had known each other for less than a week, although unbeknownst to us our lives had been entwined long before that, through Moose Schmidt. But in that week we had lived a lifetime, a whole story, and this moment, making love, with the moonlight casting a silver sheet over us, felt like the culmination of all that had gone before. It felt like the end of the story, and that was why it was so powerful, and so good. The sadness would come later.

Afterwards we lay in each other's arms and a while later I felt Jia drift on into sleep. The moonlight shifted across our bodies and worked its way very slowly over the floor of the hut.

I closed my eyes, not worrying about sleep. Sleep would come or it wouldn't. I was happy in the moment, although somewhere inside I was anxious, too. Anxious about what Moose Schmidt had said when he thought we were going to die. The more I thought about it, the more I felt Jia was right – it had simply been Schmidt enjoying some extra cruelty, trying to eke every last ounce of suffering from the trap he had led us into. I thought of One Leg, too. He believed he may have killed Schmidt. One Leg had already taken on a kind of supernatural status in my and Jia's minds. We had spoken about him outside earlier. The way he had lived for so long after taking a bullet that would have killed most men – *any* man – instantly. The way he had been able to ride a horse so easily again after not being able to ride for years – although I insisted that was down to Jia and her needles, not to some mystical Indian ability. Then there was the smoke he had raised during his war dance. It had told him something and that something had been the truth. If a man like that believed he had killed Moose, then surely he had? Although the more I thought about it, the more I thought that if that been the case then wouldn't One Leg's last words have been more definitive?

So I was a little anxious, but the wonder of my time with Jia over-rode it all.

Then something made me open my eyes, and as they adjusted to the darkness, I saw a face looking in the hut window.

It took me a moment or two to realize what I was seeing. By the time the image made sense, the face was gone. It had been a man, a young man, I was sure of that, even though the face had been silhouetted. Had he seen us? He must have done, although the beam of moonlight had cycled across the hut floor and was no longer resting on Jia and me.

I wanted to jump up and rush outside, but I was naked. My gun was somewhere on the floor.

It took me a minute to slip out of Jia's arms without waking her, to pull on my breeches, grab my gun, and get outside. The door hinges squeaked and I glanced back but Jia never woke.

There was no one within the square made by the huts.

I ran around to the back of the hut where the window was, ratcheting the hammer of my gun with my thumb as I went. Stones cut into the soles of my bare feet. The cold night air raised goose bumps on my naked chest.

There was no one there.

I moved left and right, looking at the angles beyond the huts. No one.

However, it seemed to me that there was dust hanging in the still air, just about visible in the moonlight, raised by something or someone that had passed through. It may, of course, have been my own feet kicking up that dust. Or it may have been imagination.

But there was something else, too.

A smell of smoke. The same smell of smoke that had permeated my hair and my skin and my clothes until I had cleaned up in Green Springs.

The smell hung in the air, very faint, but very real.

I wondered, for a brief moment, if it had been One Leg. Maybe he was still looking over us and his very soul was forever tainted with smoke.

But no, such thoughts were just a reaction to the conversation that Jia and I had had earlier, when we had made One Leg out to be some kind of mystic.

This smoke was real.

I walked to the edge of the huts and looked out towards the south where we were heading. There were low hills and distant rises. There were silhouettes of trees and the sky was heavy with clouds that took just that moment to obscure the moon. I couldn't see anyone.

It didn't mean they weren't there.

I circled the camp and looked in all directions.

No one.

By the time I got back to our hut the smell of smoke had vanished from the air, carried away by the cool night breeze. If, I thought, it had ever been there.

But I didn't get to sleep that night.

# 13

I saw the ghost of my father once when I was fifteen. Or rather, I *heard* my father's ghost. I was hunting up in the Blue Hills with that old musket. It was slow to load, like my pistol had been before I started using the paper cartridges, and so I tried really hard to kill whatever it was I was hunting with my first shot. That day I'd hit a small white-tailed deer and I knew it was a killing shot. The deer was less than a fifty yards away and went down instantly. It wasn't big, which meant I would easily be able to carry it home. Our neighbour Mr Young had a smoke house and Emmett Thackeray just a little further along the street always salted his venison. My ma would cook some as soon as we had butchered the animal, and so between us all, that little deer might last a while. Even if it never lasted, a few people in St Mary's would eat well for several days. Hell, I'd probably make a few dollars, too.

I was about to stand up from my hiding spot and

go and check the kill when I heard my father's voice, as clear as if he was standing right next to me, saying '*Don't move, Cal.*'

I went cold. The voice was so clear, and so close, and without a shadow of doubt it was my father. The breath caught in my throat and my heart paused, and then raced forwards. I froze, and it was a moment before I could physically turn towards the voice.

I don't know what I expected to see. We had buried my father the year before. I'd seen his body, cold and pale and thin, looking much older than he had been in life. He had appeared smaller too and although one of the bullets had hit him in the eye, it had left most of his rugged and handsome features intact. There was no case of mistaken identity. But that voice behind me had been as real as the musket that I still held in my rigid grip.

So I turned really slowly and, of course, I was alone.

I had positioned myself inside the shadows and cover made by a boxwood bush, some wild ivy, and the trunk of a cedar tree. The deer hadn't been able to see me, but I could see out all right. I could see the ground all around me, the trees, the leaves, the red dirt track that the deer had walked along just moments before.

My father was not there.

Yet the voice had been real. At the time I had no doubt about it.

I recall breathing through my mouth. I remember trying to calm myself, trying to understand what had just happened.

Most of all I recall not moving. My father's instructions had been clear. *Don't move.* So I didn't. As I tried to understand what had just happened, I also kept looking, checking every inch of the landscape all around me. I could see the deer's carcass, lying on the ground, that white tail still visible. My gunshot had caused a few birds to erupt from the trees. Any, and all, other creatures in the area had frozen or darted into hiding places. Nothing moved, including me.

How long did I wait? It felt like forever. I started to get cramp in my legs and my arms and in the end I did have to relent and very, *very* slowly adjust my position. Clouds moved across the sky.

The light changed. Birds returned and started chattering again. I saw a red squirrel scramble up a tree.

And after forever two men emerged onto the track.

I didn't recognize them, but they had revolvers drawn and they were hunkered down as if they were expecting another gunshot. They were both quartering the landscape, looking every which way.

'Reckon he's gone,' one of them said, his voice carrying on the gentlest of breezes. He was dressed in a long dark coat and a matching hat. He had a beard.

'Why would you shoot a deer and then go?' The other said. His hair was long, over his collar, and he wore a yellow hat.

'He ain't waiting. Nobody can wait that long.'

Beardy kicked the deer carcass. Yellow Hat was turning, still quartering the ground. At one point he looked directly at me, and as he did so he paused. I held my breath and after a moment his gaze moved on.

'Let's take the meat and go,' Beardy said. 'Least we eat tonight.'

Yellow Hat nodded, but continued nervously looking around. Still holding his gun at the ready, he waited whilst Beardy hoisted the small deer over his shoulders and together they walked off down the trail and disappeared.

I have no idea who they were or what would have happened had they seen me. The fact they waited for so long before breaking cover suggested that they were waiting to surprise whoever had shot the deer. I can't imagine they had been planning on a friendly surprise.

As the years went by I wondered if maybe I had heard the men, even subconsciously, and generated the warning myself.

But I could never convince myself of that explanation. My father's voice had been as real as the last time he had said goodbye to Ma and me and headed off to Fort Smith.

The reason I tell the story of my father's ghost is

that he never gave me a warning as Jia and I rode into St Mary's Gap that morning. Maybe he had been dead too long, but a warning would have been nice.

# 14

The early afternoon sun blazed down upon us from a cloudless sky. There was little breeze and the dust our horses raised made my throat and my eyes gritty. I was thirsty and I was tired. We hadn't tried to avoid the heat today. The ground was hard and as my horse trotted forwards each step vibrated up into my own body and in my weariness I started to worry that when I had last loaded Jia's gun I had forgotten to leave an empty chamber. Had I mistakenly counted and loaded five – as it would have been on my gun – and inadvertently not left a safe chamber? I knew it was nonsense, of course. I had revolved the cylinder afterwards, as I always did, and left the gun safe. I was worrying over nothing. It was just exhaustion and a worrying kind of day.

There were two horses tethered on the rail just along from Ma's boarding house. That wasn't unusual and in itself it wasn't worrying. The riders may have been talking to Ma about rooms, or they may have been in the feed store just down the road.

Or in the saloon across and down a little.

But I kept seeing that face looking in the hut window at me. I kept feeling the dust hanging in the air, smelling the smoke.

I had pushed a little harder this morning and Jia had asked why. *Just keen to get home*, I'd told her, but it was clear that she sensed how uneasy I was. We were close enough now, had learned enough about each other, to know such things.

We looped our own horses' reins over the rail and we went into the house.

Ma's front door opened into a small hallway. The hallway ran down to the kitchen at the far end, with a door on the right into a parlour and living room. The stairs to the first and second floors went up to the left. The kitchen was where Ma spent a lot of her time when she wasn't tidying up after her boarders.

The front door squeaked as I opened it but the house was quiet inside. Too quiet, I thought, as if the house had heard that squeak and was now holding its breath.

I couldn't help but think of that house in Mustang.

I slipped my Colt from its holster.

I looked at Jia and I raised a fingertip to my lips. We could be quiet too.

She drew her revolver, too.

We walked slowly down to the kitchen, treading softly so our hard heels didn't click on the wooden floor. If my mother was sitting at the kitchen table reading a book then our entrance with guns in our hands might prove a little dramatic, even embarrassing. But there was something about the stillness of the house that warranted the drawn weapons.

In the kitchen there was a big iron pot of soup bubbling gently on the stove. It smelled good – potatoes and onions, I figured. The back door was open and the breeze felt stronger and cooler here in town than it had felt on the ride in.

Nash Lane was dead on the floor.

His throat had been cut and his eyes were wide open in surprise, as if he hadn't believed whoever had done this to him was capable of such an act. Knowing Nash, I wondered if he may have been trying to create a reason for a fight the way he had with me. Maybe whilst he had been waiting for their reaction to his provocation they had simply stepped forward and run a blade across his neck. Nash had slid down the wall, knocking over a chair as he died. Blood had soaked his shirt front, and his trousers, and had started pooling around the floor where he lay half propped against the wall.

I didn't have to get too close to see that the blood was still wet. It glistened in the summer sunlight coming through my mother's kitchen window.

I heard something creak in the room above. Ma's room.

I heard footsteps up there.

Despite all that we had been through, I think this

was the worst, most frightening, moment. Not for me, not that I was scared for myself, but this was my mother's house. I was suddenly terrified of what I would find upstairs. I now understood why Jia had not hesitated when she thought the man lying on the bed in that house back in Mustang had been the man that had shot her mother in the back.

Jia was staring at Nash Lane.

I gently placed my hand on her cheek and I turned her head away from him and towards me.

*I'll go first*, I mouthed, and I stepped around her and went back along the hallway, still treading quietly. I climbed the stairs as softly as I could. Jia was behind me. I could hear her breathing.

The door to my mother's room was shut.

The door to Amos Bowler's room was open.

Amos lay half in and half out of his room. The hat that gave him his name was across the other side of the landing. It didn't take a genius to picture the hat rolling over there after they had killed him. Amos, like Nash Lane, had a look of surprise in his dead eyes. His shirt front was drenched in blood too. His throat was intact, but the very quick glance I gave him suggested he might have been stabbed in the heart, or belly. Or both.

*Jesus*, I whispered, not sure if it was a prayer or blasphemy.

I stood still and listened.

I fancied I could hear someone breathing in my mother's room, but it may have been the wind through the boughs of the oak tree out back. It may have been Jia behind me. It may even have been me. I wasn't sure.

What I was sure of was that I had to open my mother's door.

My mother had a simple iron latch on her room door, but she had a bolt on the inside. I reached out and raised the latch slowly with my left hand – I still had my Colt in the other – knowing that lifting the latch on the outside was mirrored by the matching latch on the inside. If anyone was watching, they would see the movement.

Once the latch was raised I pushed the door as softly as I could, testing to see if it was bolted.

It was.

I took a deep breath.

I let the latch back down and I stepped backwards.

I looked at Jia, held her gaze for a moment, then I kicked the door with the flat of my boot so hard that the wood shattered and the door flew open and hit the inside wall with a sound like a gunshot.

Then I was in the room, gun raised, instantly seeing the awful scene in front of me, raising my gun and ratcheting back the hammer.

Moose Schmidt was over by the window, grinning. He had a gun in his hand. His stick was resting against the wall. My mother was on her bed, and I saw ropes knotted around her wrists and then tied to the top of the bedstead. She had been stripped to her underclothes and one of her eyes was already swelling and colouring where someone had punched her.

She looked at me and I just had time to see her shake her head, *no*, as I turned my gun to kill Moose Schmidt.

But someone hit me hard on the side of the head, harder than I'd ever been hit before, and my legs folded beneath me and I crumpled helplessly to the floor, desperately trying to hold onto my vision and my gun, but failing, the darkness coming over me, my Colt clattering to the floor.

It could only have been seconds, but when I came round Jia was in the room too. Her small gun was in the big hands of a young man, a boy really, who looked too much like Schmidt not to be one of his sons. Jia was standing against the wall to my right as if ordered to do so. I'd been dragged forward a couple of feet and the door was pushed to behind me. Not that there was anyone else alive in the house to come in.

I groaned. It felt like the bones on the side of my head were broken. I had a vision of the skull being caved in and a slow painful death imminent. It certainly felt like it.

Schmidt, over by the window, was still smiling as everything had gone right to plan. Sunlight illuminated one side of his face and shadowed the other, making him look grotesque.

He saw my eyes open.

'My timing was pretty good,' he said. His illuminated eye was bright blue and as evil as anything I'd ever seen in my life.

I pushed myself up onto all fours. I felt like an old dog struggling to rise in the morning.

Schmidt's son kicked me in the side, the point of his boot like a blunt knife in my kidneys. I groaned and went down on my belly again.

My mother said, 'Someone will kill you for this.'

Jia said, '*I* will kill you.'

Moose Schmidt laughed.

'No one's managed to yet, young lady. Most of all you.'

I started to rise again, looking warily at young Schmidt. I saw that he had a knife in the belt of his trousers. I thought of Nash Lane and Amos Bowler. I thought of the surprise in their eyes. Young Schmidt made to kick me again and I winced in advance and braced myself. My kidneys felt as crushed as my skull did.

'Let him get up,' Moose said. 'I want him to watch.'

Young Schmidt took a few steps back over towards his father, in his hand Jia's gun was still trained on me. The slightest adjustment and the barrel would be pointing at Jia. Moose was still aiming his gun at my mother, despite her helplessness.

My mother told Moose how evil he was, using a

139

swear word that I'm not sure I'd ever heard her use before, and Moose laughed again. Jia told him that she knew men that would love to meet him, and that probably would meet him one day. 'You will die screaming,' she said. Moose laughed at that, too.

I made it to all fours, and then to my knees, as if praying. I looked across to Jia. Our eyes met. I couldn't read much into her expression but there was defiance there, and hate. And something else, too. Something that she had learned when fleeing from the soldiers that burned women in China. Something that had kept her alive all across Europe and in the cold, damp, hungry London nights. It was the thing that had helped her cross an ocean and then, on her own, a continent. It was a determination to do whatever was needed.

I waited for the pain in my stomach and my head to ease. It didn't. The movement had made me nauseous. At least that feeling passed.

I eventually managed to stand up, reaching behind me for support against the wall. I saw my gun, it was on the floor by Moose Schmidt's feet. I caught my mother's eyes. There was defiance and hate and determination there, too.

'It's OK, Cal,' she said. Maybe she had seen some defiance in me, also, or at least the tensing of muscles, for despite everything I was getting ready to make a move for my gun.

'You know, I never had anything against any of you,' Moose said. 'In fact I quite liked Samuel. Out of all of them he came closest to, you know, bringing me in. But he was . . . well, he thought he was in control, but he wasn't. Not even for a little while.'

Something suddenly occurred to me. I looked from Moose to his son. There was a coldness in the boy's eyes that scared me. Somehow I knew just how much he had enjoyed killing Nash Lane and Amos Bowler.

'Was it you?' I said. 'Was it you who had the gun hidden in his pants?'

But even as I said the words I knew it couldn't have been. It had only been four years before and the boy in question had been very young according to One Leg's telling of the tale.

The boy glared at me.

'He doesn't speak,' Moose said. 'But no, it wasn't him. I have a few sons. Fact is, I have more than a few.'

'God help us all,' my mother said. I'd noticed how she had been twisting her wrists and hands against the ropes that bound her, but now she went still, just as Moose looked at her.

'You know, I would've probably forgotten you had I not kept hearing how this one here was coming after me.' He turned to me and sneered. 'If his father couldn't catch me then what chance his runt?'

Young Schmidt smiled. He mightn't be able to talk but he wasn't deaf. He still held Jia's gun and I couldn't help but think he was longing to use it.

Although from what I'd seen elsewhere in the house I suspected he'd enjoy using his knife more.

'Yeah, I kept hearing how Callum Johnson was going to come after me. Oh, I was so scared,' Moose mocked. 'Year after year I was scared.' Now he looked at me. 'But you never came, did you? Seemed to me like you never had the courage. Then this one comes along . . .' He looked at Jia and he smiled. He seemed to lose his train of thought for a moment. I could see from his eyes that he was thinking of something else entirely. He looked at his son, 'She's pretty, yes?'

His boy nodded and smiled. His tongue flicked out lizard-like and left his lips wet.

Jia spat on the floor.

'He likes them lively,' Moose said to her.

'I'll cut his bits off,' Jia said.

'You'll be tied down, like Mrs Johnson here.'

Despite all the pain that was still raging in my head and in my belly, I was about ready to make a dive for the gun that was still on the floor.

'Cal,' my mother said, sensing I was at the point of doing something stupid.

'And you can watch,' Moose said, looking at me. 'How does that sound?'

'I'll kill you,' I said.

'Of course you will.' Moose's shoulders rocked with laughter. Spittle sprayed from his mouth.

I saw my mother working the knots again and one of them, the one that bound her right hand – the hand nearest Moose – appeared to be coming a little loose.

'You killed those men downstairs,' I said, looking at young Schmidt, knowing he couldn't answer. I just wanted them both to look at me. Give Ma whatever time and space I could.

But they didn't look at me. They were both looking at Jia.

She had slipped an arm out of her jacket, which was now off one shoulder. Her shirt beneath was damp with sweat and moulded to the shape of her breasts. She slipped the other arm from the jacket and let it fall to the floor.

'Take me first,' she said, looking young Schmidt in the eye. 'There's no need to tie me down.'

He looked briefly at his father and back at Jia. She reached up and undid a shirt button. Then another.

I wasn't sure what was happening, what her plan was. But I sensed it was all about getting young Schmidt worked up enough that he lost concentration and control. Maybe I could help.

'You saw us, didn't you?' I said to him. 'Back at the camp out of town. You looked through the window and saw us lying together.'

Jia glanced at me. I'd never mentioned the face at the window to her.

'Did you like what you saw?' I asked him.

He made a sound that wasn't even close to speech. It was animal-like.

'Jia,' my mother said. 'You don't have to.'

But Jia was holding young Schmidt's gaze. She had undone all but one of her shirt buttons and now she pulled her shirt out of her trousers. Her stomach was flat and smooth, the skin glowing with dampness.

Young Schmidt looked at his father again. Moose was grinning. He said, 'You all know that you brought this on yourselves. You started it, is what I mean.'

Young Schmidt looked back at Jia.

Jia lifted a leg, reached down, and slipped off a boot.

I wanted to tell her to stop, that maybe there was another way, but she wasn't looking at me. Her eyes were still fixed on young Schmidt, and his on hers. It reminded me of the moment she and One Leg had connected during the break at the bird fight. A message that no one else could hear was passing between them. I could see young Schmidt breathing harder, a flush working its way up his neck. His nostrils flared and he blinked rapidly as if he had sweat in his eyes.

Jia slipped off her other boot.

'Hope you know what you're doing, young lady,' Moose said, still smiling. 'He likes to do it with a knife in his hand. And afterwards, if he ain't pleased, well, you know.'

But she ignored Moose and she undid her belt, letting the leather ends swing loose. Then she

144

started to unbutton her trousers.

'Come here,' she said to young Schmidt.

Now he broke the connection between himself and Jia and he looked at his father. 'Give me the gun,' Moose said. 'And keep your knife handy, like you did for all the others. Just don't use it too soon.'

Moose looked at me and smiled as his son handed him the gun. Now Moose had a revolver in each hand. None of us – my mother, Jia, or I – were armed. Moose said, very matter-of-factly, 'If he doesn't enjoy it, he kills them afterwards. Sometimes he kills them even if he likes it. I think if he likes it he gets jealous thinking of other men who may enjoy the girl in the future. So he kills them. The way a child's brain works, yes?'

'You're a monster,' I said.

Jia held her arms out wide.

'Come on then, child,' she said.

Young Schmidt made that animal sound again, he breathed in deeply and swelled his chest. I was still standing against the wall by the broken door and young Schmidt would have to walk right by me to get to Jia.

Moose read my mind.

'You try anything and I'll shoot your mother. Jakob's good with the knife and he's also the strongest boy I've ever seen at his age. Stronger than most men. Strong as an ox, in fact. So you try anything and he'll most likely gut you. But I'll still shoot your mother. And that still leaves the China girl.'

Jakob Schmidt walked right by me, not even sparing me a glance, and I could smell the lust upon him as he started to unbutton his own pants.

'Jia,' my mother said.

'Come on,' Jia said to Jakob. 'I'm waiting.'

Jakob grunted something.

Moose said, 'He wants you to step out of your trousers.'

Jia did as she was instructed.

I had to use all my self-control not to reach out and grab Jakob, to pull him away from Jia. His trousers were around his ankles and his knife was in his left hand. Jia was reaching out towards him, pulling him close as if she wanted to embrace him.

In the last moment before he pressed his lips upon her she caught my eye and I received her message as loud and as clear as that time my father had spoken to me from beyond the grave.

*Now,* Jia said. *Now's the time.*

Moose was laughing. Outside a horse neighed and that too sounded like laughter. I heard people talking from across the street. A dog barked somewhere further down town. I heard my mother sob.

Jakob made an animal sound again, this time from deep down in his throat.

I don't know what Jia did to him, but one moment he was pressing himself against her, doing something between them with his right hand whilst his left held that knife, ready to plunge it into her if she didn't please him, and then I saw her reach up to his neck with her left hand, press her thumb into his neck, and he simply slumped against her, all that ox-like strength vanishing instantly.

Where Jia got her strength from I don't know, but she caught Jakob and she held him like a shield. There was a moment when she eased the pressure on Jakob's neck and I thought he stirred, but I couldn't be sure about that, for by then Moose had realized that something was wrong, that his son was unmoving and silent. Moose swung one gun toward Jia, lifting it slightly where he had unconsciously relaxed his aim, only to discover that he daren't pull the trigger because Jakob was covering Jia.

It was a split second but it was all I had. It was all I needed.

I launched myself at Moose and hit him around the waist just as he twisted and fired one of his revolvers. The explosion was deafening within the room. I felt the bullet slice through my flesh like a great needle. I felt the heat, the punch, the immediate wetness.

And I thought of One Leg surviving for however long it took to do what needed to be done after he'd been shot.

My momentum smashed Moose up against the window frame. Glass shattered. I'm sure there were yells of alarm outside. I grabbed Moose the way Nash Lane had once grabbed me, a bear-hug, holding him as tight as I could, not letting him get his hands up and point either gun at anyone.

147

Although his hands were trapped between us, he pulled the other revolver's trigger, and this time the explosion was muffled between our bodies. I felt a burning sensation on my thigh, but whether it was from the gunpowder discharging inside the gun or the bullet itself I wasn't sure.

I hauled Moose upright from the window, intending to throw him down on the floor and kick him, stomp him, do whatever I could. I knew he had a weak leg and I was sure I could take advantage of that. I felt him release one of the guns that was caught between us and I felt him trying to work his now free hand across to the other gun, to pull back the hammer. I squeezed him tighter trying to prevent his hands moving between us. If I released the bear hug for even a second he would have the advantage.

For a moment our faces were inches apart. His beard smothered my mouth. I could smell his breath; taste the foulness of his lips. It felt like I was an inch away from kissing the Devil. Our eyes met. His looked black, not blue, this close. He was breathing heavily as if he'd been running, wheezing and choking.

But he was strong. Stronger than I would have imagined.

So I squeezed harder trying to stop that breathing altogether, but he grinned at me and I felt him finally cock that hammer between us, maybe with his thumb rather than his free hand. He squeezed the trigger again. I felt the burning of the gunpowder blast and this time I felt a bullet plough into my thigh.

It was like being kicked by a horse and my leg folded beneath me. There was nothing I could do. I was helpless and in that second he knew it, and I saw him grinning as my grip loosened.

I heard more shouting from the street outside.

Moose Schmidt raised the revolver, reaching up with his free hand to ratchet back the hammer. His eyes locked on me, his grin widened.

Then I saw my mother sitting up on the bed behind him, her left arm still bound to the bed, but her right arm free and holding the loose end of rope.

A split second before Moose Schmidt pulled the trigger, my mother wrapped that free end of rope around his throat and yanked him backwards.

Moose wasn't expecting it and I think he was balanced on his bad leg.

He squeezed the trigger by reflex as my mother pulled him towards her. The bullet whistled past my face. Off balance and with no strength in my leg I fell against the window frame. Moose landed on top of my mother, face upwards, and I saw her immediately twisting her hand so that the rope wound around her own wrist, pulling it tighter and tighter around Moose's neck.

Moose, lying on my mother but staring up at the ceiling, levered the hammer back on his gun, raised the gun, and pointed it vaguely backwards. He fired and the bullet embedded itself in the wall behind the bed. He tried again and this bullet blasted into a pillow and feathers exploded outwards.

The third time he managed to twist his hands such that the gun barrel was pointing directly at my mother's face.

She was pulling the rope as tightly as she could, using every ounce of her strength. All of Moose's body weight was on her. His mouth was wide open and his cheeks and the skin around his eyes was bright red. I saw Jia across the room dropping Jakob's unconscious body to the floor.

I wanted to get across to the bed, to knock that gun from Moose's hand, but as I pushed myself away from the window frame my leg gave way totally.

Moose pulled the trigger on his gun. The hammer fell on an empty chamber.

It was Jia's gun. Had Moose been expecting six shots? His eyes widened with fear and panic. The gun had been his last chance.

One of those eyes suddenly filled with blood.

He dropped the gun and started clawing at the rope. But he couldn't get his fingers between the hemp and his own throat. His hands dropped away, seemingly of their own accord, and he started thrashing wildly on the bed. It seemed impossible he wouldn't break free of my mother's one-handed hold.

Then Jia was on the bed, too, kneeling beside my

mother, reaching down below Moose Schmidt's neck, finding my mother's grip on the rope.

Jia added her strength to that of my mother and together they pulled the rope tighter. Together they held it tight.

I saw Moose's remaining good eye fill with blood.

It was a long time after he had stopped thrashing, after he had stopped moving altogether, that Jia and my mother let go of the rope.

# 15

By the time Jakob Schmidt came round to find himself tied up with the same rope he and his father had used on my mother, the room was full of townsfolk. Our marshal – Vincent Jenny – had taken control. He, like everyone in town, like Moose Schmidt himself, had been aware that one day I was planning to go after Schmidt. Vincent knew who Schmidt was, and what he had done.

Someone fetched the doctor – Andrei Mikhailov – and Andrei examined my mother and Jia and then me. He told me I'd been shot twice. I said I reckoned I could be a doctor because I knew that already.

He said I was losing a lot of blood.

I said I knew that already, too.

He asked me what I thought he ought to do about the bullet wounds, if I was such a good doctor.

Apparently, I never answered. I passed out.

We had a new judge in the territory. A handsome man who wore a fine suit and was well groomed. He had arrived about the same time as Jia. Isaac Parker was his name, and by the time Marshal Vincent Jenny delivered Jakob Schmidt to Judge Parker, our new judge had already found fifteen men guilty of murder. In time, young Schmidt would be the sixteenth.

My mother told Jia and I how the Schmidts had arrived just as Nash Lane had finally had enough of her saying no to him and, according to Nash, belittling him.

'It was the Devil and the deep blue sea,' my mother said. 'Nash let himself into the house, came into the kitchen, and told me that enough was enough, that I'd been teasing him for too long. He was drunk, but I knew this time he was serious. I think the fight with you last week pushed him over the edge. He wanted to get back at you as much as he wanted to rape me.

'He didn't notice the Schmidts come in behind him. The young one – Jakob – walked up to Nash and cut his throat. Just like that. For about one second I was thankful – and then I realized that I'd been cast into the hands of devils.'

My mother looked at Jia as she spoke.

'He told me they'd killed you. Both of you. Said he'd burned you both to death. I was devastated.

After that, I didn't care then what they did to me. Or at least I didn't think I cared. Once they started . . . .'

'He just wanted to make the moment worse for you,' I said. 'That's what he does . . . what he did.'

'When you kicked in the door . . . .' My mother shook her head. There were tears in her eyes and on her cheeks.

We were in the kitchen. My mother, Jia and I. My leg was bandaged – both legs. My torso, too. I'd lost a lot of blood but I was lucky according to Andrei. Three bullets over the last few days, he'd said, and no damage. I told him I didn't feel lucky and he said what did I know, I wasn't a doctor. A couple of my mother's friends had helped scrub the blood from the floor in the kitchen, on the landing, and in the bedroom, and when I was stronger I would fix the bullet holes and the window.

Jia and I told my mother what had happened in the few days we had been gone. We told her about One Leg and about the fire. We didn't tell her about us – but I think she knew.

At one point Jia mentioned the vision her mother had had about killing Moose Schmidt. 'It was that vision that gave her the courage to go after him,' Jia said. 'In the vision . . .' she paused. 'In the vision she strangled Moose with a rope. That's why she wanted to get so close to him.'

My mother said, 'It was you, wasn't it? In her vision? You look like her, I'm sure.'

'Yes,' Jia said. 'It was me. I know that now. The

154

vision was true.' Again she hesitated and I could see in her eyes that she was wondering if her mother had had to die after all. Then she said, 'But maybe it had to happen this way.'

We drank some whiskey – all of us – and we toasted Samuel Johnson and One Leg Hawk. We toasted Yellow Jack, Liu and Chen. We toasted Yu Yan, Jia's mother.

Then Jia drank all her whiskey in one go, put her glass down a little heavily, and told us tomorrow it would be time for her to go home.

I loved her, but it had never been, could never be, anything more than what it was. I guess I had always known that, although I had probably refused to accept or believe it. Jia had wanted, and had needed, revenge. As did I. As, it turned out, so did my mother. Together we had all played our parts.

The morning she left, I walked Jia to the livery and I helped her with her horse. We brought the saddled horse outside and we stood next to it, Jia holding the reins. The vast horizon and deep blue sky over her shoulder looked too big to me. New York was so many thousands of miles away that it seemed impossible that this girl, on her own, on a horse, could ever get there.

'It will be easier than what we've done this last week,' she said.

'I'd be happy for you to stay,' I said. 'I would love for you to stay.'

She smiled.

'I could love to stay, too, Cal. But it's not our destiny.' She took my hands in hers. Her skin was warm and soft and I felt tears in my eyes and a massive sense of coming loss in my heart. '*Yuánfèn,*' she said.

'You told me,' I said. 'It's fate that we found each other.'

'It can mean that. But it can also mean more. It can mean fate without destiny.'

'Fate without destiny?'

'It means we were right to find each other at the time we needed each other, but we are not destined to stay together.'

'All in one word?' I said, feeling that coming loss creeping closer.

'Yes, that's the beauty of our language.'

'I should learn it,' I said, forcing my lips into the shape of a smile.

She smiled too, but didn't tell me that my learning her language was a good idea.

'You have family?' I asked. I knew that she did. Aunties and uncles, cousins. We had spoken of such things in our time together the previous week.

'Yes. And you have your mother and I've been in St Mary's Gap long enough to see there are lots of pretty girls.'

'None like you.'

'And you're handsome when you smile.'

She let go of my hands and suddenly that loss felt

real, as if it had arrived deep inside me with the force and suddenness of an unexpected clap of thunder. It hurt more than my bullet wounds.

Then she put her hands on my shoulders and she kissed me on the lips.

'I will never forget you,' she said. 'Or your mother or One Leg. Thank you for helping me.'

'Thank you,' I said.

'Don't cry,' she said.

'I'm not crying.'

Then she smiled one last time, climbed on her horse and rode away, leaving me alone in the street, feeling as if I was the last one standing in the whole world.

My story doesn't end there, although you could argue that story does. A week after we had killed Moose Schmidt – who had already come to be known as the Monster of the Territories – I rode, freshly bandaged, to Fort Smith to see Judge Isaac Parker.

It took three days of waiting before I gained an audience with Parker – and to this day I believe that delay was a test of my determination. But eventually I sat down with him in his office and we drank tea and I told him my story. I told him of my father, and I told him of One Leg Hawk and of Lin Wu Jia, and I told him of Moose Schmidt. He already knew about Moose Schmidt, of course. By then Jakob Schmidt was already in a cage somewhere in Fort Smith.

When Parker asked me why I had come, why I was

I telling him my story, I looked him in the eye and I said, 'I would like a job, sir. I believe you're hiring deputy marshals to police the Territory.'

Outside Schmidt's office, and across the yard, they were building the huge scaffold that would come to be infamous in due course through all the multiple hangings that would occur there.

Judge Isaac Parker looked at me and said, 'You went after and killed the monster, yes?'

'Not just me, sir. I had help.'

'I know. You were very gracious and complimentary about them in your telling of the story.'

'They deserve it.'

'Could you have done it on your own?'

I wanted the job. I had come to realize that my destiny, my own *Yuánfèn*, was to honour my father and continue his work. That's what he had trained me for – without my realizing it until these last few days. And thus, I wanted to answer 'yes' to Parker's question. But I knew that he would see through the lie.

'No sir, I couldn't have done it on my own.'

He nodded.

'You said your father travelled with a Cherokee scout?'

'Yes sir. One Leg Hawk. *Tawodi.*'

'You speak Cherokee?'

'No sir.'

He smiled. 'I like you, son. You're more honest than most I take tea with.'

'Thank you.'

'You'll probably die out there. You know that?'

'I'll do my best not to, sir.'

He paused. I paused. Eventually, in the gap, I asked, 'Does that mean I have the job?'

He picked up his cup, realized it was empty, frowned and put it down again. He looked at me, although it was more studying me than merely looking at me. 'I know someone who could use a little help out there this summer. It'll give you chance to see how you like it.'

I could tell from his expression that what he really meant was that it would give *him* chance to see how *I* did.

'Thank you, sir, I won't let you down.'

'I'm sure you'll do your best not to.'

'Who is this person?' I asked. 'Where do I find them?'

'He's probably in the saloon right now. You can't miss him. He's a tall man with a big moustache and a suit almost as nice as mine. He'll probably be playing cards. My advice is not to play cards with him.'

'I'll go and track him down,' I said.

Parker smiled. 'He probably won't be happy with me sending him an assistant. But tell him you're the one that killed Moose Schmidt. He'll be impressed.'

'Thank you, sir.'

'One other thing. He's black. I'm guessing you won't have any issue with that, on account of Lin

159

Wu Jia and *Tawodi*. Seems to me you get on well with all colours and creeds.'

I was impressed that he had remembered One Leg's and Jia's names. But I didn't say that to him. He knew it was impressive anyway.

'Yes sir,' I said.

'Good. Welcome on board.'

He stood up and held out his hand. We shook and his grip was firm. As was mine. And that was how, the summer after we had killed Moose Schmidt, I ended up riding the Territories with Bass Reeves.

But that's another story.